S0-BBF-454

In memory of Atlas

BOOKS BY DR. HARPER

I'm a Therapist and My Patient is Going to be the Next School Shooter

6 Patient Files That Will Keep You Up At Night

I'm a Therapist and My Patient is In Love with a Pedophile

6 Patient Files from Prison

I'm a Therapist and My Patient is A Vegan Terrorist

6 Deadly Social Media Influencers

The Disturbing Incidents at Lonesome Woods Boarding School

Return to Lonesome Woods

THE
DISTURBING
INCIDENTS
AT LONESOME
WOODS
BOARDING
SCHOOL

DR. HARPER

This is a work of fiction.

Names, characters, businesses, places, events, locales, and incidents are either the products of the author's imagination or used in a fictitious manner.

Any resemblance to actual persons, living or dead, or actual events is purely coincidental.

Copyright © 2021 Dr. Harper

Book Cover Design by ebooklaunch.com

All rights reserved.

ISBN: 0-578-98664-7
ISBN-13: 978-0-578-98664-7

"Have I gone insane?"

"No, Elliot… But you may have to choose between two realities."

Samantha from Durham UK
I travelled a long way to visit and it did not disappoint. This boarding school is as haunted as it gets!

INFECTIOUS

I wasn't always like this, you know — paranoid, temperamental, vindictive.

I mean, sure, I've always been a bit... high strung. But I never used to stalk my therapy patients. Or yell at them. Or hold them captive in my garage.

No, all of that started *after* the incidents at Lonesome Woods Boarding School.

And I'm not talking about the school shooter.

This was something far more insidious — something... infectious. Like a cancerous disease that tore through the student body, rotting young hearts one by one.

But mental illness can't do that.

Can it?

I came into this profession optimistic and ready to help. I was young, naive, and eager to find the glimmer of good in every patient.

But after Lonesome Woods, I began to search for evil instead.

Kelley from Winchester
Thank you for showing us around! It was very informative to learn the history of what happened here. We really appreciate you allowing us to spend the night due to the storm. Can't wait to get home and tell everyone about you and this place!

RAIN

The strange rumors of Lonesome Woods Boarding School spanned back decades.

Reminiscent of a small college, the grass-and-brick campus housed students from all over the state — except the town in which it was built.

The people of Lonesome Woods never wanted a private school in their once-protected wetlands. They fought its founding. They fought its construction. They fought its opening.

But they were no match for the out-of-state cash that poured into the project, so eventually they gave up their fight.

Or so the school thought.

Spend one evening at a dive bar downtown, and you're guaranteed that a local drunk will proudly tell you about the rain.

Yeah. The rain.

With only 82 days of precipitation per year, Lonesome Woods was one of the sunniest places in the country — except the school.

Tucked away in an isolated valley a few miles from downtown, the school seemed to be socked into a perpetual state of meteorological misery.

Truly, I cannot remember that last time I saw the sun shine

from my office window.

But it's not just bad weather, according to the townspeople.

No, if you ask them, the rain is cursed.

I know it sounds ridiculous, but over the years, the school *has* seemed to suffer a disproportionate share of... unfortunate incidents.

Disappearances, fires, floods, and even murders.

I've looked into all the stories, and every single one can be traced back to logical, rational explanations: accidents, relationship drama, and the most dangerous culprit of all: teenage angst.

And of course, correlation does not equal causation. Perhaps the Homicidal Prom King and Queen of '08 lacked adequate vitamin D levels. And maybe the infamous Graduation Day Suicide Pact of '09 was really just a multi-patient case of seasonal affective disorder. And the deadly Dormitory Collapse of '15? I mean, what do you expect when you build a school on top of a swamp?

But despite endless practical answers, "cursed rain" is what the media decided to go with.

The rumors started years ago, after the headmaster's son went missing. He declared the rain "cursed and evil", and the townspeople loved it. They genuinely believed that their town was defending itself from wealthy urban invaders. It got to the point where pastors were leading prayer services to call upon this sinister rain.

Stories eventually began circulating online, and that's when the school picked up national notoriety. Horror fanatics bussed in from all over the country to take pictures of the bad weather. Someone opened up a museum downtown to profit from the school's sordid, drizzly history. Parents started pulling their kids out of class based on the 10-day forecast.

Eventually it got to the point where the school started having enrollment issues.

So over the years, the headmaster adopted a more secretive approach to addressing these issues. Towering granite walls surrounded the campus, locking students safely inside the gloomy fortress. Threatening signs appeared for miles along the winding dirt road to the school, warning tourists to turn back or face legal consequences. Phones were forbidden on school grounds, even for faculty members. And rather than involving local authorities in the school's private matters, the headmaster decided it would be better to start handling things internally.

And that's why he hired me.

Because of rain.

I was having trouble finding work as a recent psychology graduate, and it seemed like an easy gig. Get paid a decent salary to talk with rich kids. Free housing, free food, and free summers. I couldn't believe such a great position had been listed for over a year with no takers.

When the headmaster gravely explained the "cursed rain" situation to me, I laughed and accepted the job because I don't believe in urban legends.

What a mistake that turned out to be.

Chelsea from Corby
I knew a girl that had a sister who went to this boarding school!!
Her sister was brutally murdered by the prom king and queen!
There's a rumour that if you go to Lonesome Woods Boarding
School on the anniversary of the prom massacre you can hear
the dead screaming and the ghosts running around, the prom
king and queen possess any human that enters to massacre even
more

FORKS

The first incident occurred at lunchtime on a predictably dreary afternoon.

I made a habit of sitting with the students at lunch. I found it easier to build a rapport with young people in a casual setting, rather than the typical couch-and-notebook power dynamic.

It took a few awkward months of eating alone, but I now had a reliable group of students who joined my table every day. And they seemed to take pride in it, as if we had formed some sort of elite club.

"What's for lunch today, Elliot?"

I insisted they call me by my first name, so that we felt like equals. The rest of the school administration hated that. They thought it was a "slippery slope" — whatever that meant.

"Boxed lunch as usual — ham and cheese sandwich," I said, turning to Allie. "I don't trust the pizza here."

"Smart move!" she said brightly. "How's your day going?"

Allie was by far the smartest person at the school, destined to become valedictorian and spend the next four-to-twelve years at an Ivy League college. She was smiling, but I quickly noticed that something seemed off. Thanks to the academic pressures of being number one, she had always been a nail-biter — but today was different. She was going at them harder than her actual lunch.

"Day has been fine," I said, unwrapping my sandwich. "Everything okay?"

"Oh!" She laughed nervously and pulled her hand from her mouth. "Yeah. Just worried about the physics test this afternoon."

"Ah," I said, taking a bite. "I'd be scared too."

Over the next few minutes, our usual gang filled the table.

"My man, Elliot!" Wyatt clapped me on the back and reached out his hand. "What's good?"

I attempted to perform our secret handshake, which I had somehow gotten worse at throughout the semester. Fortunately, his hands were as strong as the rest of his body, so he guided (or forced) me through most of it.

"Didn't see you at the game last night," he said. "Are we in a fight?"

I laughed. "Sorry, the school governors called a late-night meeting."

"Mhmm…" he mumbled, digging into his food. "A likely story. Breakin' my heart, Elliot."

He was joking, but he was right. I wasn't being honest. There had to be *some* boundaries between us. The truth was, I was on a date last night, and it didn't go well. It turned out the gay scene in Lonesome Woods was… well… it was exactly what you might expect from a small town that prayed for cursed rain.

"Greetings, all!" Oliver sat down across the table and sipped water from a long straw that came from his backpack. "What news does the day bring?"

We're not supposed to play favorites, but if I did, Oliver would be my favorite.

Scrawny and straight from the 19th century, he was… unique. Sporting his usual survivalist gear, Oliver was prepared for a catastrophe at any turn. I'm not really sure what sort of disaster he was anticipating at a gated private high school, but no one could deny that he was ready.

At first, the school administration thought he might be a "sightseer", which was their fancy word for "crazy horror enthusiast who applied to the school to experience its morbid history first-hand."

That's why they asked me to keep tabs on him. But as I quickly discovered — and reported back to them — Oliver wasn't here as a tourist. Oliver was just... different. And he was probably on the spectrum.

I'm glad they put him on my radar though. Before our little lunch club, I'm not sure he had any friends at the school. In addition to his unusual demeanor, his strawberry blonde hair and freckles became the target of some nasty bullying. Now he had a few friends to stand up for him.

"Ollie!" Wyatt reached out for the handshake, which Oliver performed flawlessly. "Greetings, noble comrade."

Oliver gave him a big smile and began reading some book about the Civil War.

Next up was an exasperated Isabelle, who Allie once described as "an exhausting mess of high heels, fake English accents, and first world problems". It wasn't a particularly nice thing to say, but it definitely covered the basics.

Isabelle blew us all kisses, and then dove straight into her complaints.

"Hello, loves. The weather here is simply dreadful," She grabbed Wyatt's hands dramatically. "Our trip to Milan can't come soon enough. Don't you agree, babe?"

"*Yes, babe*..." Wyatt, Allie, and Oliver droned in unison.

Isabelle and Wyatt were a natural pairing — popular girl and athletic jock. But if you asked me, I got the sense that Wyatt might be more interested in Oliver.

Who knows, though. Like everything else gay about me, my gay-dar expired when I moved to Lonesome Woods.

Last to the table with nothing but a bag of salt and vinegar chips, was Kat.

"Whaddup, daddy?" she ruffled my hair in a harder-than-friendly way. "What happened to your hair? Looks like shit today."

We're not supposed to have least favorites either, but Kat would definitely be mine.

Reminiscent of a grade school bully, Kat's self-described greatest strengths were 'eyeliner and the ability to knock bitches down a peg'. On top of that, she insisted on calling me "daddy" ever since my failed attempt at learning more about her father and childhood.

"I told you not to call me that—"

"Hey kids." Kat ignored me and squeezed in between the others. "What has he diagnosed you with today? Let me guess… Anxiety, narcissism, autism, and… hmmm… let's say, alcoholism."

Everyone looked up from their food in annoyance — except Oliver, who appeared confused.

"Who's who?" asked Oliver curiously. "Isabelle is of course the narcissist…"

"Excuse me?" Isabelle crossed her arms.

Not one for picking up on social cutes, Oliver continued: "And after Friday night, I must assume Wyatt is the alcoholic—"

"Thanks for that, buddy."

"Which leaves anxiety and autism…" Oliver tilted his head, deep in thought. "While I *do* experience intrusive thoughts from time to time, I wouldn't necessarily categorize it as 'persistent worry', which is a key symptom of anxiety. And if you look at the technical definition of the disorder, I'm actually a bit more—"

"Autistic!" Kat threw up her hands. "You are *aggressively* autistic."

"Knock it off," I warned Kat.

"Autistic, of course." Oliver nodded and returned to his book. "That makes more sense."

I would report Kat for bullying if she wasn't so damn insecure. The others were used to her comments by now anyway. And even though she would never admit it, I knew the lunch crew gave her a sense of belonging. Why else would she willingly sit here every day?

For the next few minutes, we listened to Isabelle recount the trauma of being cut off from her dad's credit card. I know therapists are supposed to be good listeners, but the story was so boring that I almost decided to wrap up lunch early.

Thankfully, Oliver interrupted her to share a passage from his book, which nobody except Wyatt paid any attention to. Wyatt didn't seem to understand a word Oliver was reading, but he asked a few questions which Oliver happily answered.

"So you see, while Gettysburg gets the most attention, Bull Run was actually the deadliest—"

"AGHHHHH!"

All six of us jumped at the bloodcurdling scream from the table next to us. Or maybe it was the table across the way? Or the table near the windows?

It took me several moments to realize it wasn't just one scream. Students all over the lunchroom were running away from their tables in horror, panicking and crying.

I stood up, heart pounding. "*What the hell is going on…?*"

My biggest fear was an active shooter situation, but as I surveyed the lunchroom, I didn't see any weapons. Instead, I saw something much more bizarre. On every single table except ours, one student stood perched. Something was sticking out from their hands — something that appeared to be dripping with blood. And they sounded like they were… chanting?

"Get out of here," I said urgently to the group. "Go get help, okay?"

They all nodded in agreement — except Allie, who was sitting there in silence.

"*Allie*," I hissed. "Go!"

She closed her eyes, trembling in her seat.

"I'm sorry," she whispered.

"For what—"

But before I could finish my sentence, she grabbed her fork from her plate and drove it through her left hand.

"Jesus, Allie!" I shouted.

Oliver tore through his backpack for bandages and leapt

across the table to help her. But she shoved him aside and slowly stepped on top of the table.

As she stood up, she held her hand in the air — fork sticking out from her palm.

And then a toneless, deep voice emerged from her mouth. Something that didn't sound like Allie at all. Something that didn't even sound human.

"Cursed be Canaan..." she chanted as blood spurted from her hand.

Speechless, the rest of us looked around the lunchroom — watching in horror as eight students held their fork-impaled hands in the air.

"The lowest of slaves will he be to his brothers..."

They were all speaking in unison.

"Cursed be Canaan."

Angela from Talladega
Thanks for letting us visit, but something felt off and spooky. As if someone was breathing in my ear. I heard silent screams in the walls "help us!" The sound of children playing in the halls but there were no children

HENRIK

"What do you mean you *don't know?*"

"I don't know!" I said, for the sixth time. "What do you want me to say?"

"I'm going to need more than that." Henrik Small — who was anything but small — stormed around the conference room. "We have eight students in the nurse's office with bandaged hands, telling us they don't remember a *GODDAMN THING!*"

The other school governors cowered in their seats as the ex-military headmaster kicked over a chair, WWE style. Clocking in at 210 pounds with a full grey beard and mustache, he was undoubtedly the most intimidating (and unstable) 60-year-old man I'd ever met.

"Well, I'm sorry but I don't have a diagnosis for self-inflicted fork wounds."

I was trying not to lose my patience, but I had to stand my ground. I got the sense he was attempting to pin the blame on me in front of all the governors (it was really just a school board, but 'governors' sounded fancier).

"Brainstorm with me then," said Henrik as the others quietly watched us argue. "Are they... Are they possessed or something?"

"What?" I stared at him incredulously. "Are you serious?"

"I don't know!" He threw his hands in the air, extending his already towering stature. "Give me a better explanation, Elliot."

"Genesis 9:20-27…" I thought out loud. "It's not exactly a Satanic ritual. It's the story of a child who was cursed because his dad saw his drunk grandpa naked."

He screwed up his face. "What?"

"Welcome to the Old Testament." I shrugged. "It has some homophobic and incestuous interpretations, but I'm more of a literal reader. Who knows, though. Maybe it was a homophobic prank?"

"Some prank!" he scoffed. "And you think Allie Pruitt would get involved in something like that?"

I bit my lip and sighed. "No… That's the problem. I don't know the other kids, but I know Allie. And she would never risk her future like that."

"So we're back to possession," he said. "Figures. Hired a therapist when we should have hired an exorcist."

"It's not possession!" I repeated louder.

The other governors raised their eyebrows. Nobody shouted at Henrik Small.

"Sorry." I lowered my voice. "But I'm sure there's some sort of psychological explanation."

"You're the expert!" he said derisively. "So what did you miss? Surely there must have been some warning signs?"

"Signs of stabbing themselves and chanting Bible verses?" I snapped. "No. I think I would have reported that."

"Watch your tone, Elliot," he said darkly. "Remember, you're here at our invitation."

"I'm sorry," I said again. "But I just need more time to talk with the students. Then I'm sure I'll have more details for you."

"Well, you're in luck," he said. "You'll have plenty of time to connect, because the governors have decided that every dormitory suite will be assigned a faculty chaperone."

I raised my eyebrows. "Chaperone?"

"That's right," he said. "Phase one of my rapid response plan: monitor and scramble all student housing assignments. No more friends and cliques and secrets. We need to get ahead of this thing."

"What? You can't make faculty members live with students."

"Check your contract," said Henrik, producing a piece of paper. "*Faculty members will serve as chaperones on overnight trips, which may require sharing accommodations with students.*"

"That's for field trips!" I said in disbelief.

"Then consider this a field trip," said Henrik. "You'll be living with your famous *Lunch Crew*, of course."

"What—"

"You've actually modeled it perfectly. A representative from each social circle — an athlete, popular girl, outcast, over-achiever, and a punk."

"Did you devise this plan while watching the Breakfast Club or something?"

He continued on, ignoring me. "Then they can report back to you regarding their people."

"Their *people*?" My jaw dropped. "They're not FBI informants! They're just kids who sat at my table."

"Well, now they're your roommates," he said simply.

"This is — You can't—" I turned desperately to the other nine governors. "You can't possibly think this is a good idea?"

They looked down uncomfortably.

"We've already taken the vote." Henrik spoke for them. "You'll move into Hopkinton Hall by supper. Unless, of course, you'd prefer to move back home?"

I glared at him and bit my tongue, trying not to say something that could cost me my job. So instead, I managed to give him a curt nod before walking out of the room.

"This is insane," I muttered under my breath as I shut the door behind me. "I am not living with Kat Bruno."

Finny from Harrisburg
Hi, Maybe someone that comes across this can help me. The Dormitory collapse wasn't an accident. I've been working on this for years and no one seems to believe me.

ROOMMATES

"No way, daddy. Top bunk is mine."

I watched in silent resignation as Kat tossed my bags on the ground. Both of us knew she would beat me in a fight.

"I hope you all don't mind, but my alarm goes off at 4:30am to begin daily preparations." Oliver made up the top bunk next to ours. "You're welcome to join me, of course."

Kat rolled over. "Ollie, dear. You know I love you, but if I hear your alarm at that hour — and this is a promise — I will murder you."

"Hmm…" He tilted his head. "I received similar feedback from my previous roommates. I suppose I could attempt to re-calibrate my internal clock?"

"Good boy." Kat rolled back and began clipping her toenails.

"It's a bit odd, isn't it?" said Isabelle, claiming the last top bunk before I could get there. "A male staff member living with us…? I mean, for all we know, he's some sick pervert or sex predator. No offense, Elliot."

"None taken…" I gave her a forced smile.

"Well I think it's cool," said Wyatt, dribbling a basketball on the hardwood floor. I would have to knife that in the middle of the night. "I see enough of the team at practice and games. It'll be fun living with you guys. Did you request this, Elliot?"

"*I most certainly did not…*" I muttered under my breath.

I was surprised to see Wyatt settle into the bunk below Oliver, rather than his girlfriend. Interesting. Another piece to the mysterious puzzle of Wyatt.

I reluctantly made my bed below Kat's pedicure shop and put my clothes away in my three allotted drawers. God, this was like college all over again. At least in college I had a triple.

Everyone went quiet and stared when Allie appeared in the doorway.

Even I had no idea what to say.

"Hello, everyone," she said meekly, arm behind her back. "Hope you're doing well. Looks like I've been reassigned to this room."

She hung her head and found her way to the bed below Isabelle's.

"How are you doing, Allie?" Isabelle jumped down and hugged her. "We've been ever so worried."

I raised my eyebrows, pleasantly surprised by Isabelle's compassionate response.

"Don't WORRY… You're SAFE with us." Isabelle continued, but her voice had become loud and slow, as if Allie was deaf or incredibly stupid. "I've hidden ALL the FORKS in our room."

"Alright princess!" Kat hopped down from her bunk and pushed Isabelle aside. "Lovely sentiment. I'll take over from here."

Isabelle shrugged. "What did I say?"

"Listen." Kat threw her arm on Allie's shoulder. "I'm fine with the chanting shit, but I was raised Catholic, so I feel it's my duty to tell you that you're headed straight to Hell—"

"Good talk, everyone." I interrupted Kat and stepped forward. "Allie, let's go for a walk."

"No, that's alright…" Allie mumbled.

"That wasn't a request," I said sharply. "Now."

The others made '*ooooh*' sounds, but I didn't care.

I had work to do.

> Xavier from Lonesome Woods
> *I survived the collapse. I can assure you it was no accident. The night it happened, I awoke to a voice whispering in my ear "and it all comes tumbling down". Still paralyzed to this day.*

SCARED

The Granite Footpath followed the inside of the entire campus wall.

It was installed just a few years ago, after various complaints that the wall made the school feel like a prison. Now they used the path as a selling point during tours, although people barely ever walked it because of the weather.

Exotic trees lined the mile-long loop, giving the school plenty of opportunities to plaster big donor names on plaques and benches.

Allie and I walked along the back wall, watching drizzle turn to stream on the pond.

"I know what you're going to ask me," said Allie. "But I don't remember."

I nodded. "That's okay."

"Really?" She raised her eyebrows. "Then why did you want to walk?"

"I needed a few minutes of quiet," I said. "Figured you could use a breather too."

"Oh." She nodded with relief. "Yes. Thank you."

We continued walking in silence. Past the outdoor swimming

pool. Past the red clay tennis courts. And past the front gates — which sometimes felt more like they kept people inside than out.

We had almost completed a full loop when Allie finally spoke softly:

"I'm so scared, Elliot."

There we go.

I slowed down and turned to her. "Scared about what?"

"It's just — I think…" Her voice trailed off.

"Allie?"

Her eyes watered. "C — Can I tell you a secret?"

"Of course," I said gently. "That's what I'm here for."

"You have to promise not to tell anyone!" she blurted out. "Not the lunch crew, not the teachers — nobody."

I nodded and held her gaze. "You have my word, Allie."

She looked absolutely miserable and broken, like she had been holding onto this secret for a long time. I felt a pang of guilt, reminded of Henrik's accusation that I didn't see the warning signs.

"So…" she sniffled. "About a month ago—"

CLANG

Allie stumbled into something, so we both stopped walking and looked down at her feet.

"*What the…*" my voice trailed off, quickly replaced by Allie's screams.

It was a pile of eight blood-stained forks.

A few steps ahead, there was a stick figure scribbled in white chalk — except the hair, which was bright red.

Below it, a simple message:

SHHHH

Taylor from Lonesome Woods
I escaped this school. No one in my new life knows this. But I'll let you all in on a little secret. Those of Lonesome Woods KNOW what is going on at that boarding school. I'll curse my parents forever for putting me through what they did.

GABRIEL

Bells jingled faintly as I stepped through the door.

My first impression was more of a small antique shop than a museum.

Dimly lit, musty, and a vague hint of patchouli everywhere.

The front desk was empty, so I started flipping through the carousel of gift cards:

HAVE A MERRY BLOODY CHRISTMAS

WILL YOU BE MY PROM NIGHT KILLER?

HAPPY GRADUATION DAY MASSACRE

"*Good lord…*" I muttered to myself. This was even more tasteless than I expected.

I wasn't exactly sure why I came here today. Allie and the other seven students were completely shutting me out, Henrik had no explanation for the forks and chalk drawing (except to 'expel the student responsible'), and I had already Googled "red-headed stick figure + Lonesome Woods" to no avail… So I guess I just didn't know where else to turn.

But looking around at the signs and exhibits in the room, I was beginning to realize this was a mistake.

ENJOYING YOUR VISIT? I'M WRITING A BOOK ABOUT LONESOME WOODS. LEARN MORE AT LONESOMEWOODS.ORG AND BE SURE TO LEAVE A NOTE IN MY GUESTBOOK.

I took out my phone to load the website, which was somehow even more campy and crass than the museum itself. I began reading through a few seriously bizarre guestbook entries:

DeShan from Smithville

During a student council meeting, I noticed their odd behavior. The eyes are what I noticed first. Slits instead of pupils! Cold. So cold were their bodies. I offered snacks, but all they could do stare. Slowly, they tried approaching; closer and closer. I backed away and ran faster than I thought possible. I don't think these students were students at all.

Ronnie

Stay Away From the Children

Jasmine from Visalia

I was going to win 2008 prom queen.. but now I keep reliving a horrible death. What happened to me? And have you seen my prom date Jorge?

Jorge from Visalia

It all happened so fast. Come to think of it, has anyone seen my prom date Jasmine?

"Disturbed?"

I jumped at the hand on my shoulder.

"*Jesus,*" I breathed and put away my phone. "Hi."

"Gabriel," said the stranger, extending his hand. "Welcome to my museum. Don't be alarmed by the guestbook entries. Some of my visitors have… active imaginations."

He was smiling at me in a relentless way that made me very

uncomfortable. It felt like he was… inspecting me.

"Elliot…" I shook his hand.

Gabriel was about my age — late twenties, maybe a bit older. Tall with dark features and a perfectly defined jaw-line, I would have described him as unfairly handsome if I wasn't so creeped out by him.

"It's a pleasure to meet you, Elliot," he said. "What brings you here today?"

"Just in town for a few weeks," I lied. "Heard good things about the museum."

"A tourist?" He raised his eyebrows. "You'd be the first in quite some time. You're aware that the school now has walls and trespassing laws? I'm unable to operate campus tours."

"Yes," I said. "I just came for the… peace and quiet."

Gabriel eyed me suspiciously. "Very well. What can I help you with?"

"Just looking around," I said. "Should I buy tickets or something?"

Gabriel smiled again and held his hands behind his back.

"For you, Elliot, it's on the house."

I looked away awkwardly. What was *with* this guy? This was worse than shopping at GNC. I shuffled sideways to escape his gaze and turned my attention to a nearby display.

STILL MISSING? THE MYSTERIOUS CASE OF TIMOTHY SMALL

"Ah, Timothy…" Gabriel swooped up next to me. "A natural place to start. The very first tragedy of Lonesome Woods Boarding School."

I sighed and accepted the fact that this was going to be a guided tour.

If I was to play tourist, I would have to pretend all of this was new to me.

"The headmaster's son. Wandered off campus and disappeared into the night during his sophomore year. But there is more to the story. You see, in the weeks leading up to Timothy's disappearance, one of his teachers became worried about him."

I raised my eyebrows. That actually *was* new to me.

"Why?"

"Bruises — all over his body," answered Gabriel. "The town and school investigated the case for a year but produced no leads. Eventually his father called off the search and held a funeral for his son."

"A funeral?" I said. "Even though they never found his body?"

"If you ask me, the old man couldn't stand the uncertainty any longer," said Gabriel. "He needed closure — especially if he was to continue running the school."

"More like controlling the school..." I muttered.

Gabriel raised his eyebrows. "You're familiar with the Lonesome Woods headmaster?"

"Oh, no—" I hesitated. "I just... I think I read it in a book somewhere."

"Ah, of course," said Gabriel, clearly unconvinced. "Yes, Henrik Small grew obsessed with protecting the students from these endless occurrences. Some say he's gone a bit mad over the years... Rumors of blackouts and dementia episodes."

I looked at the display in front of us. Photos of Timothy from school — an awkward looking kid with red hair, a mole on his left cheek, and ocean-blue eyes behind a pair of glasses. Age progression pictures showed unsettling renditions of what he might look like now. Still awkward, but a bit thicker with receding auburn hair.

Finally, a map of the school's campus traced six different paths she could have followed into the woods that night.

"It looks like one of those detective boards," I said. "I'm assuming you think he's still alive?"

"I'm not certain either way." Gabriel paused for a moment. "But over the years, there have been stories of Timothy making... appearances at the school..."

"What sort of appearances?"

Gabriel thought for a moment and then nodded.

"Come with me."

He touched my arm gently, and I felt a surge of nervous

excitement course through my body.

What in the world was that?

I followed him to a small room in the back — past some more bleak displays, and a table of water-filled jars labeled *100% LONESOME WOODS RAINWATER*.

"Timothy has been known to leave messages around the school…" said Gabriel, digging through a cardboard box in the middle of what appeared to be his bedroom. "They don't allow cameras — or me — in the school anymore, but here is the last known sighting."

Chills ran down my spine as I looked at the photo he handed me.

A familiar red-haired stick figure, and a message scrawled in chalk:

HELP ME

"*Shit…*" I whispered. "Is that the Granite Footpath?"

Gabriel glared at me and took the photo back.

"For a tourist, you sure seem to know an awful lot about the school…" He stepped closer to me and ran a finger along my cheek. "Who are you, Elliot…?"

I began to panic, realizing how much trouble I would get in if the school discovered I was at the museum. Why the hell had I given him my real name?

"Sorry," I said, backing out of the room. "I — I have to go."

"Wait," he said, trailing after me. "Elliot."

Heart pounding, I was practically running for the front door. All I wanted to do was get out of this morbid, depressing place — away from morbid, depressing Gabriel.

As the bells jingled, Gabriel called after me one more time. "Elliot!"

Against my better judgment, I turned around and took a deep breath.

"Listen, I really have to go," I said. "Thanks for the tour. I can pay if you want—"

"I already told you, it was my treat," said Gabriel, eyes flickering with… desire? "And if you'd allow it, I would love to treat you again — perhaps to dinner this weekend?"

My cheeks went pink. I certainly wasn't expecting *that*.

"*No, thank you*," said my brain. "*You are a walking red flag of darkness and mystery.*"

Unfortunately, my less intelligent organ spoke for me.

"S — Sure."

> Lindsay from Memphis
> *Curse this school. I'm still looking for my sister.*

TIMOTHY

"You haven't been honest with me, Henrik."

"I beg your pardon?"

We were alone in the headmaster's office, and I needed answers.

"You never told me about the other drawings — about who they *clearly* represent."

Henrik's face went pale and his expression hardened.

"How dare you bring Timothy into this."

"I'm not trying to be disrespectful," I said carefully. "But Henrik, you asked me here to keep the kids safe. How can I do that if I don't have the whole story?"

"You're a glorified guidance counselor, not a detective," Henrik spat. "*I'LL* decide what you need to know."

"But the chalk drawings—"

"Have you been in town?" demanded Henrik. "Gossiping with the local vultures?"

I sighed. "Yes. Okay? I went in town to clear my head. I'm being honest with you, and I need you to be honest with me. Could Timothy be drawing those chalk pictures?"

Henrik glared at me, eyes bulging as if his head was going to explode.

"Follow me, Elliot," he said, heading for the door.

I shut my mouth and trailed after him. As we made our way

through the halls, I realized we were headed straight for the front entrance.

Well. That was a short-lived job — even shorter than my brief stint as a waiter. How was I going to explain this on a resume? Maybe I wouldn't even bother listing it.

But to my surprise, Henrik walked outside in the rain with me and stormed toward the faculty parking lot.

"Get inside," he commanded as we approached an old Prius.

"What?"

"Now." He pulled himself into the driver's side and looked comically large inside the car.

I hesitated for a moment and then joined him on the passenger side.

"Where are we going?" I asked quietly as he started driving.

He didn't answer.

As we made our way through the front gates and through the dark wetlands of Lonesome Woods, I began to feel more and more nervous. This wasn't normal, right? Driving off into the middle of the night with the notoriously unstable school headmaster?

My heart sank further when we slowed down in front of a cemetery.

"Henrik…" I said. "I'd like to go back to school now."

He ignored me again and turned off the car.

"Out."

I closed my eyes and took a deep breath. "Henrik, whatever you're thinking—"

"OUT!" he barked.

I nodded and shoved the door open, stepping back out into the rain with him.

He walked past several graves before slowing down in front of one small tombstone. I joined him and waited for my eyes to adjust to the dark. Then I made out the engraving:

TIMOTHY SMALL

No years. No message. Just his name.

"I may not have his body, but Timothy is dead," he said, voice cracking. "This godforsaken school stole him from me.

Everything you've heard about Lonesome Woods is true. The place is cursed. It has been cursed since the day he went missing."

I raised my eyebrows. "Then why do you stay?"

"It's all I have left," he said. "I lost my son. My wife left me. This school is all I have, and I am determined to put an end to this curse — or whatever you want to call it. That's why I hired you. That's why you're living with the kids."

"Do you really think it's cursed?" I asked. "I mean, what if there are logical or psychological explanations for everything?"

"It's cursed," he said definitively. "I'm as logical a man you'll ever meet, but I've seen more people die at Lonesome Woods Boarding School than all of my assignments overseas combined. The longer you stay here, the more it will consume you."

"What do you mean?"

"The nightmares will start soon, if they haven't already," said Henrik. "Before long, you'll struggle to untangle dreams from reality. Now is the time to save yourself, Elliot. You can leave if you want — get far away from this miserable place. No one will blame you."

"I'm not leaving," I said gently, undaunted by the supernatural. "I want to help — if you'll let me."

Henrik's expression finally softened a bit.

"The chalk drawings are a prank," he said. "I promise you. Just sightseers — trying to get a rise out of me."

"So install some hidden cameras along the Granite Path," I suggested. "I can send you a few recommendations."

"Fine," he said. "Anything else?"

I had one more question, and I needed to approach it delicately.

"Before your son went missing — or passed away — I heard he might have had some... bruising on his body?"

Henrik nodded.

"Timothy was an unusual child," he said. "And the other children were unkind."

"Bullying?" I asked.

"It's my best guess," said Henrik, gazing sadly at the

tombstone. "That's why I said goodbye to him out here. Far away from the school, so at least his memory could live in on the sunshine. And what do you know? The goddamn rain followed him out here."

"I'm sorry, Henrik," I said softly. "For everything."

As we stood there together in the graveyard, I could have sworn I saw a tear run down his cheek.

Then again, maybe it was just the rain.

Sam from Ogden, UT
Interesting way to kill an hour or two...I don't know there's some
weird vibes...like you can feel the pain and fear? I... I wish I
hadn't come.

BLOOD

Several nights later, I returned to the graveyard with Gabriel.

"A cemetery..." said Gabriel. "It's not exactly the first date I envisioned."

"I need your help," I said, making my way back to Timothy's tombstone with two shovels.

Something had been eating away at me all week, and I had to find answers.

"Why did you bring shovels, Elliot?"

Gabriel's face glowed in the dim moonlight, making him even more distractingly beautiful.

"We need to dig up the grave," I said.

Gabriel raised his eyebrows. "Now it's *definitely* not the first date I envisioned."

"I have to know why Henrik held a funeral for a son whose body was never found," I said. "Please, will you help me?"

Gabriel's dark brown eyes flickered with a familiar hunger. "Yes, Elliot."

We got started, shoveling dirt and moss to piles on the side.

It was hard work — harder than it ever looked on television. Before long, both of us were sweating in the cold night air.

Gabriel pulled off his shirt, revealing a slender but incredibly toned, smooth body — glistening with beads of sweat and rainwater. My face went red with embarrassment as he pulled off my shirt to reveal my skinny, un-muscled body.

But self-consciousness quickly turned to excitement when he put his shovel down on the ground and stood behind me, pressing his naked torso against my back.

"Now it's a date," he whispered into my neck, guiding my arms as I shoveled. His forearms and biceps flexed with every movement.

I wanted so badly to give in to the temptation — but first I needed answers.

So we kept digging, deeper and deeper, until finally we heard the *thud*.

We tossed the shovel aside and got down on our knees, brushing dirt aside until the coffin was fully exposed.

"*Shall we open it now…?*" whispered Gabriel, running his tongue along my neck.

"Yes," I said, heart pounding. "I have to know."

I felt Gabriel's teeth sink into my neck, but for some reason it didn't hurt. If anything, I wanted him to go deeper. So he did.

"*Open, Elliot…*" he whispered, kissing me with lips that were dripping in my own warm blood. "*Open…*"

As we made out in the moonlight, I reached forward and lifted the top off the coffin.

"*Look, Elliot…*"

Lips locked together, we looked down into the coffin.

"*Look…*"

I tried to scream, but nothing came out.

Laying there inside the coffin, was the most horrifying thing I had ever seen in my life.

Kevin from Trebbin
I can still remember seeing this place in the news. It was a report about the classroom fire that killed the 5 kids. I came to get my kid and seeing the parents of those children cry... I thought about that for a long time.

WORSE

"Are you okay?" Oliver stood over me with a look of deep concern. "You were screaming and you're perspiring heavily. And you appear to have an erec—"

"Jesus!" I rolled to the side and yanked a blanket over my body. "Go back to sleep!"

"No offense," came Isabelle's voice. "But shouldn't a therapist be the one helping *us* with nightmares?"

To my horror, I realized that all five of them were standing around my bed.

"Everyone back to sleep!" I barked from under the covers. "It was just a bad dream."

"Wish *my* bad dreams were like that..." Wyatt smirked.

"Am I the only one who actually feels *less* safe with our faculty chaperone?" Kat chimed in.

"BACK TO SLEEP!" I shouted.

All of them wandered back to bed — except Allie, who just stood there staring at me.

"Allie, I'm fine," I said. "You can go back to sleep now."

"They've started, haven't they?" she whispered.

"What?"

"The nightmares," she said robotically. "They'll only get worse from here."

Chills ran down my spine. For some reason, it almost sounded like a threat.

We looked at each other in silence for several more moments.

Then she broke into a smile and walked away.

Samantha from Pulaski
It smelt like fire the whole tour. If I didn't know any better I would've thought the building was going up in flames

WOUNDS

Sitting across from Gabriel at dinner, I found myself unable to make eye contact with him after my dream. So instead, I was downing waters as fast as the waitress could bring them.

"You can relax, Elliot," came Gabriel's calm voice. "Nobody from the school will see you here."

I looked up. "How did you—"

"Telepathy," he said. "One of the many powers we vampires possess."

I accidentally spat out some water. "You — what?"

Gabriel gave me a strange look. "That was an attempt at humor… I searched your name online and you're listed in the school's faculty directory."

"Oh," I said, trying to compose myself. "Yes, sorry. I was just trying to stay under the radar."

"A wise decision." Gabriel nodded. "The school has never taken kindly to my museum."

Thankfully the waitress came back to refill my water again, which I promptly began chugging.

"Now, if I was a therapist…" said Gabriel. "I might think you were a bit nervous tonight. Would that be an accurate diagnosis?"

I took a deep breath and tried to look at him without imagining him as a half-naked vampire.

"Y — Yes. Sorry."

He reached out and gently touched my water-glass-gripping hand.

"You have nothing to apologize for," he said soothingly. "May I hold your hand?"

I finally let go of the glass and held his hand — which immediately sent shockwaves of anxiety and arousal through my entire body.

The joys of being a nearly-30-year-old virgin.

"What's on your mind, Elliot?" His eyes gazed straight into my soul as he slowly massaged the top of my hand with his thumb. "What brings you to therapy today?"

I looked up and finally managed to crack a smile for the first time.

"Just things at the school." I sighed. "Things I probably shouldn't talk about."

"Our session is confidential." He smiled back at me. "Nothing you say will be repeated — or displayed in my museum."

I laughed. "It's just… Odd things are happening — things I can't explain with psychology. And since I don't believe in curses, I'm at a bit of a loss on how to help the students."

"Must they be mutually exclusive?"

"What do you mean?" I asked.

"Curses and psychology," said Gabriel. "I've always seen curses as nothing more than dark energy that lingers after deep psychological wounding."

Now this was a conversation I could get into.

"What type of psychological wounding is strong enough to stick around like that?"

Gabriel thought for a moment. "The dark triad."

I frowned. In the psychological world, the dark triad referred to three dangerous personality traits: narcissism, Machiavellianism, and psychopathy.

"What do personality disorders have to do with it?" I asked.

"No, no." Gabriel shook his head. "The *spiritual* dark triad — betrayal, abandonment, and rejection. The excruciatingly painful events that disconnect the human heart from God's love. The fall from grace."

I raised my eyebrows. "You're spiritual?"

"Of course," said Gabriel. "I believe that God flows—"

"Through all of us…" I finished quietly.

"Precisely." He smiled and held my hand tighter. "But intense trauma can sever that connection — and until the disconnect is resolved, there will be turmoil."

"And that's what you think is happening at the school?"

"Yes," said Gabriel. "That is why I founded the museum. To give a voice to the lost souls that wander the school — begging to be acknowledged and welcomed back into the great connection."

I nodded, speechless. This was already the most interesting date I had ever been on.

Ring! Ring!

"Shit—" I reached into my pocket to grab my cell phone. "Sorry, it's the school. I have to take this."

"You have nothing to apologize for," said Gabriel again.

I thanked him and answered the call.

"Hello?"

"Elliot." It was Henrik. "We have a situation. Where are you?"

"I'm — out for a walk," I lied. "What's going on."

"Get back here," he said. "Now."

"Wait, Henrik, what's—"

But he had already hung up on me.

"Is everything okay?" asked Gabriel.

"No." I shook my head and grabbed my coat. "I'm so sorry to do this, but they need me back at the school."

"You must stop apologizing for things you cannot control," he said, standing up and walking me to the door. "Thank you for your time this evening."

"I'm so sorry, Gabriel," I said as we stood out in the rain

together. "I'll — I'll pay you back for the check."

"Yes… All those waters were quite expensive."

I laughed and finally looked directly into Gabriel's mesmerizing brown eyes.

I wanted him to know this wasn't some kind of bail-out tactic. I wanted him to know that I liked him. But I was too cowardly to tell him — so instead I just kept apologizing.

"I'm really sorry," I continued babbling on. "I was having a great time. The conversation was—"

"Elliot…" To my shock, Gabriel leaned in and kissed me. "I like you very much."

My heart lit up as he backed away slightly and smiled at me.

Finally, I had a risk-free opportunity to share my feelings too. A chance to tell him how much I enjoyed our short date. A shot at returning his kiss and passionately making out with an incredibly attractive, intelligent man.

Instead, I managed to stammer "th — thank you" as I reached out to shake his hand.

Jesus, Elliot. No wonder you're a virgin.

> Lauren
> *This was meant to be a day out at a museum with my family ..*
> *that's not how it turned out*

SEVEN

My heart sank as I pulled into the school's entrance.

Red and blue lights illuminated the buildings, and sirens blared in the distance.

I parked the car and ran over to a crowd by the south side of the Granite Footpath.

I quickly identified Henrik's giant body in the sea of people and pushed my way to him.

"What's going on?" I asked, out of breath.

"Look up, Elliot."

I frowned. "What?"

"UP!" Henrik pointed to the top of the granite wall, which towered at least forty feet above us.

I finally looked up and realized why everyone was standing here.

I counted twelve students — all standing side by side at the top of the wall with their hands behind their backs. I recognized eight from the lunchroom incident, including Allie. The other four were new faces.

"*What the hell…*" I muttered. "What are they doing?"

"You tell me, Elliot," said Henrik — then he screamed to the side: "WHERE IS THE GODDAMN FIRETRUCK? WE NEED A LADDER, NOW!"

"I'm thinking of a number between one and twelve…"

The students were all chanting again, but this time their voices were high pitched and playful — like children playing a game.

"They've been saying that for fifteen minutes," said Henrik. "What does it mean?"

"What?" I said. "How am I supposed to know what that means?"

"Pick a number, father…" they chanted.

Henrik went red in the face and stormed away. "FIRETRUCK!"

I wandered closer to the wall, standing alongside several police officers who also seemed at a loss.

"I'm thinking of a number between one and twelve…"

"Allie," I called up. "Talk to me, please."

She didn't look at me.

"Pick a number, father…"

"I know you were trying to tell me something the other night," I said. "I want you to know, you can trust me with anything. I promise, Allie, I can keep you safe."

Finally, she looked down at me.

"The firetruck is almost here," I said reassuringly. "We'll help you down. Then I'll help you through all of this. I'll keep you safe."

"I'm thinking of a number between one and twelve…"

"SEVEN!" came a drunken shout from a group of snickering athletes.

"NO!" I cried, spinning around. "SHUT THE HELL UP!"

But it was too late.

I watched in horror as the students began pulling pieces of paper from behind their backs — from left to right, one by one — and holding them out for us to see.

"TEN"

Read the first student. She giggled and threw it to the ground.

"TWO"

Read the next student. He folded it into a paper airplane and tossed it into the night sky.

"EIGHT"

"ONE"

"SIX"

"THREE"

The ritual continued on until it was Allie's turn.

"Allie!" I called up again desperately. "You don't have to read that. Just throw it behind you, okay? Just toss it right to the ground."

I could see her hands shaking from all the way up there.

But she didn't listen to me. She took the paper from behind her back, read it, closed her eyes, and held it out for us to see.

"SEVEN"

All of the students on the wall started clapping excitedly. "*Yay, father!*"

"Allie, please…" I pleaded, sensing something terrible was about to happen. "The firetruck is almost here."

Allie took a deep breath — teetering back and forth on the edge.

"SEVEN TIMES, FATHER!" she shouted.

And then she jumped.

Maire from Mansfield
I've got a bad feeling, I'm no stranger to that, but something here just feels wrong.

BEWILDERED

"A GIRL IS DEAD!" came Henrik's shouts from the conference room. "ELEVEN MORE COULD HAVE DIED!"

I eavesdropped as Henrik tried to convince the governors to have all the children interrogated by police detectives.

"IT'S FOUR MORE STUDENTS THAN THE LAST INCIDENT!" Henrik's voice boomed again. "THE CURSE IS SPREADING AND IT'LL KEEP SPREADING UNTIL IT KILLS THEM ALL."

He sounded completely insane, even from out here.

They argued for what felt like an hour, before finally taking it to a vote.

I couldn't quite make out the final tally, but based on Henrik's shouts, I could tell they decided against it.

I heard some smashing and slamming from the room, and then the door swung open — nearly hitting me in the face.

"ELLIOT!" he barked. "WHERE WERE YOU TONIGHT? A GIRL IS DEAD! ELEVEN MORE COULD HAVE DIED!"

I stared at him.

"WELL?" he demanded.

"I — I was right there with you," I said, confused. "You were the one who called me there. And you asked me to wait outside while you spoke with the governors…"

He glared at me and then nodded.

"Of course," he said, breaking into a brisk walk. "Well, off to the dormitory with you."

"I actually have some thoughts," I said, trailing after him. "About tonight. I'm wondering about the number seven… Possibly seven deadly sins? And the whole father thing—"

"Elliot, now is not the time," he said. "Return to your dormitory."

"But you told me to wait—"

"NOW!" he shouted.

I watched, bewildered, as Henrik stormed down the hallway and kicked over several extremely expensive decorative pieces while screaming about the curse.

As much as I dismissed the idea of a curse, I couldn't actually think of any possible answer as to why twelve students would be jumping from walls and stabbing themselves with forks. And to make matters worse, the numbers only seemed to be growing — and the incidents only seemed to be escalating.

So if it wasn't a curse, what in God's name was happening to these students…?

Jeep
Electricity went out within ten minutes of arriving. Some members of our group began experiencing thoughts that could not be explained no matter how you tried. One of the men began singing in an odd high-pitched voice sitting alone near the far corner. His voice was normally deep and manly but sounded like a woman singing. I am not sure what happened. I will not be returning.

ENGLISH

When I returned to the room, the others crowded around me.

"What's happening, Elliot?" asked Isabelle. "Did Allie survive?"

I shook my head sadly. "I'm so sorry."

"Fuck," Kat whispered, an uncharacteristic expression of vulnerability in her eyes.

"Oh my…" said Oliver. "I'm very sad to hear this."

I realized one of them was missing and quickly scanned the beds to see Wyatt laying alone on his bunk with a bottle of wine.

"Wyatt, you can't have that in here."

He stared up at me miserably. "Seriously? After what we just saw?"

I sighed. "Fine. Just… Drink some water too, okay?"

He grunted and returned to his bottle.

"Listen," I said to all of them. "I'm here to talk about Allie any time you need. But I'm also here to talk about other things, okay? I need you all to be honest with me. No matter what you're going through, I promise I will keep it secret and help you."

They all nodded — for once, without any snark commentary.

Wyatt looked up from his bottle and blinked a few times, like he wanted to say something. Then he leaned back and took another swig.

"Something is clearly afoot," said Oliver, taking out his flip notepad. "Tonight I counted eleven of my peers. The fork incident was only eight."

"Yes," I said. "Whatever it is, it's spreading. So I need all of you to be on high alert."

"We want to help," said Isabelle determinedly. "Allie was one of us."

"Agreed," said Oliver. "We are at your service."

Kat nodded. "What he said."

"Well," I said. "I'm going to start with a walk — on the Granite Path. You're welcome to join me. We could all use some fresh air and exercise before bed."

Truthfully, I was going out to look for more chalk drawings. But it couldn't hurt to have some more time to talk with them, especially after what happened.

They all nodded eagerly and grabbed their coats, except Wyatt.

"Wyatt, are you coming?" asked Isabelle.

"I'm good," he mumbled.

So the four of us wandered out into the stormy night.

The police had cleared out, and I knew Allie's body was already long gone.

Without all the sirens and commotion, it felt eerily quiet.

As we walked the loop, Oliver occasionally broke the silence with facts about the plants and trees that we passed. I found it strangely soothing.

We slowed down as we approached the crime scene from earlier.

The whole section of the footpath was still roped off, so we detoured onto the grass.

Then we slowed down and stood there together, paying quiet respects to Allie.

"Oh god, what is that?" Isabelle abruptly ended the moment and pointed inside the sectioned-off zone. "Is that — is that her blood?"

"No." Kat rushed ahead and ducked under the rope. "It's some sort of drawing."

Heart racing, I stepped up to join them.

There it was — same as the others. Red-haired stick figure, this time with a new message:

ENGLISH

"English...? What the hell does that mean?" Kat asked for all of us.

I frowned. "I... I don't know."

"The little stick boy is downright creepy, isn't he?" said Isabelle.

"Looks a bit like Ollie if you ask me," said Kat.

Oliver nodded. "The resemblance is uncanny."

"Come on..." I said. "Let's keep moving."

I'd gotten what I came here for. Another message with zero clues. *English?* What did that have to do with anything? English, the subject? English, the language?

"I'll be right with you," said Isabelle softly. "I'd like to pay my respects."

I nodded, finding myself increasingly surprised by Isabelle's more sensitive side.

But as we started walking away, Oliver turned back and jogged up to Isabelle.

"What is that?" he asked.

"Nothing," said Isabelle, pushing him away.

"Is that a phone?" Oliver persisted. "Those aren't allowed on school grounds."

I ran up to them and grabbed it. How the hell had she gotten this in here?

On the screen was a photo reel. It started with pictures of the chalk drawing, but as I scrolled up, I saw images from earlier in the night — of the students on the wall.

And finally, a video... of Allie's jump.

"Isabelle, where did you get this phone?" I demanded.

"I just picked it up—"

I grabbed her by the collar, which was the first time I've ever grabbed anyone like that.

The others stared at me, frightened — but I was not going to let another one of them die because I let them keep secrets.

"Tell me now," I growled. "Where did you get the phone?"

Isabelle began crying and looked at me pleadingly.

"A man!" she stammered.

"WHAT MAN?" I shouted back, right in her face. "TELL ME HIS NAME."

"The owner of the museum downtown!" she sobbed. "Gabriel."

Tamera from Wooster
This is a very interesting place, many of the children were so helpful and very considerate when I got turned around and lost during my visit. Although I still can not find my way out.

CREEP

"Excellent work, Elliot!" Henrik boomed as the others waited outside his office. "God, how did I miss this? Of course it's that creep."

I nodded, although the word "creep" made me wince — even though it was my initial impression of Gabriel too.

"Apparently he provided Isabelle with the phone in a detection-proof lockbox," I said. "That's how she got it through security."

"We'll adjust security protocols first thing in the morning," said Henrik. "So why is he doing this? Trying to boost slumping museum sales?"

"Maybe," I said, careful not to betray my closer knowledge of Gabriel. "It could just be his interest in the school. Apparently he asked her to take photos of anything 'unusual'. $100 per photo."

"$100?" Henrik scoffed. "Isn't her family rich?"

"Her father recently cut her off from his credit cards," I said. "It sounds like she was trying to make some money on the side — to fund her online shopping addiction."

"Oh, Gabriel is going to pay for this..." said Henrik. "The damage he's done to this school... I've been trying to nab the little creep for years, and now we've caught him red-handed."

"What are you planning to do?" I asked.

"Well, we already banned him from school grounds years ago," said Henrik. "And now I'll call the school's lawyer and the police."

"The police?" I felt my stomach turn. "Do you really think that's—"

"Necessary?" Henrik raised his eyebrows. "Can you imagine if that video made it online? The trauma it would cause to Allie's grieving family?"

"Right…" I said. "Right, of course."

I knew he was right, but some part of me still felt guilty for acting so quickly, without verifying any of the information.

But that was probably my own personal biases coming into play. I was still grappling with the fact that the first guy I had developed feelings for in a long time was involved in this. Thankfully it was barely half a date, so it wouldn't take long to get over it.

"By the way," I said. "Can you check the cameras and see who did the drawings tonight?"

"I haven't had them installed yet," said Henrik.

"Are you serious?" I said in disbelief. "They arrived last week."

Henrik glared at me. "In case you haven't noticed, I've been somewhat busy…"

I sighed and shook my head. "*Unbelievable.*"

Henrik frowned. "What's unbelievable?"

I stared at him. "The fact that we don't have cameras installed yet."

"What are you talking about?" said Henrik vacantly. "What cameras?"

Jenn from The Asylum
*Every time I reach the exit, I'm back at the entrance with a
horrible new tale to follow. Who would ever wish to leave this
wonderfully terrifying place?*

GOODBYE

A few days after Gabriel was brought in for questioning, I
found the courage to return to the museum. I wanted to leave it
alone, but I couldn't stop thinking about him.

I had to confront him. I had to get answers.

But when I stepped through the jingling doors, all I found
was scattered cardboard boxes in an uncomfortably hot, empty
room. The air conditioning must have been broken.

"We're closed," came Gabriel's voice from the small
bedroom in back.

I wandered back to see him sorting through piles of photos.
To make an awkward situation even more awkward, he wasn't
wearing a shirt. And he looked exactly like the Gabriel from my
dream.

"I said, we're closed—" He looked up. "Oh. Elliot."

I took a deep breath, trying not to stare. "What's going on
in here? Why is everything boxed up?"

"I'm closing the museum," he said.

"Why?" I asked. "Weren't you cleared by the cops?"

"Yes, but the school is suing me for reputational damage."
He stood up, revealing a lean, sweaty set of abs. "And while I

don't believe they would win that case, I don't have the resources to fight them."

"Oh."

I couldn't think of anything else to say.

"You need not worry, Elliot," said Gabriel. "I didn't mention your name to the police. You and I never went on that date."

My heart churned — a sickening mix of guilt, anger, and… longing.

"Why did you do it?" I blurted out, unable to decipher my feelings.

Gabriel raised his eyebrows. "Excuse me?"

"Why did you give her that phone?" I said. "She's a child! Allie was a child. I get that you have a business to run, but involving children?"

"I didn't do this, Elliot." Gabriel looked tired. "But I suspect you already know that, or you would not be here."

"How else would she know your name?" I countered. "She's not exactly the type to frequent museums."

"Isabelle has spent a lot of time here over the years," he said. "She was one of my most loyal customers, long before she enrolled in the school."

"What?" I laughed. "Isabelle? That's ridiculous."

"I'm not going to defend myself, Elliot. I already spent two days in an interrogation room. But be careful with Isabelle Carnegie. She is not the wealthy ditz she pretends to be."

"What are you talking about?"

Gabriel looked at me one last time, and then returned to his boxes.

"I have a lot of packing to do."

The agitated sensation in my heart felt even worse than before.

"So that's it?" I said. "We're just… we're done?"

"I tend not to battle fate," he said. "I've taken all of this as a sign that it's time to move on."

"Move on?" I repeated. "From the museum? From the town? From me?"

"Yes," he said, yanking some tape across the top of a box. "I think I'll move back to the city."

As he continued packing, I felt my eyes start to burn. I knew the conversation was over, but I couldn't stop looking at him. It was almost hypnotizing to watch his arms and shoulders move as he worked. A methodical combination of grace and strength — like a spider spinning its web.

He let me stare for a few more moments, and then he closed the box.

"Goodbye, Elliot."

> Ava from Lonesome Woods
> *stay far away from this place, they want you to visit but what ever you do DO NOT COME NEAR if you ever wish to leave again*

FEEDBACK

Belle's Blog of Horrors
SPECIAL EDITION - INSIDE LONESOME WOODS -
PART 6

Good morning, fellow horror fanatics! I know you've been waiting for an update. First off, thank you for ten thousand followers! This has been my most popular series ever.

I have to lay low for a while because the headmaster has lost his mind after the latest incident. It's a witch hunt around here.

I can't get into too many details, but a student died last night. She jumped from the Granite Wall after chanting a numbers game with eleven others. The curse is definitely spreading, and it has the school panicked.

Timothy is back, and they know it. He won't rest until every one of us is dead.

Laying low until the next update. Tell all your friends to subscribe!

* * *

Henrik's face went livid as I scrolled through the blog for him.

There were photos from all around the school — including the fork incident. Isabelle was careful never to include herself in the pictures. Just enough to prove that she was there, giving the people an exclusive lens inside Lonesome Woods.

"SIGHTSEER!" he pointed and shouted at my computer screen like a madman.

"Exactly," I said. "It's Isabelle. So you can tell the lawyers to leave the museum alone now."

Henrik frowned. "Why would I do that?"

"Because he didn't do anything!" I said. "She lied."

"How do we know this is Isabelle's blog?"

"Seriously?" I threw my hands in the air. "Belle…? Isabelle…?"

"That's not proof of anything," said Henrik. "We can't just go around making accusations."

"That's what she did to him!" I looked at Henrik in disbelief.

"That creep had it coming!" He slammed his fist against the wall. "Unless you have some proof, the lawsuit will proceed as planned."

I glared at him, furious.

But if he wanted proof, I would get him proof.

* * *

"You called for me, dear?"

"Yes, please come inside," I said, ushering Isabelle into my office.

She put down her purse and took a seat. "What's going on?"

I turned my computer screen around to face her, and then I loaded her blog.

I watched closely for some sort of reaction, but she gave me nothing.

As I scrolled through the entries, Isabelle stayed quiet the entire time — eyes moving rapidly back and forth, like she was playing some sort of chess game with me.

"You can't prove it." She finally spoke, and her fake accent was gone. "Or Henrik would already have expelled me."

I took a deep breath, trying to stay calm.

"Isabelle, you're profiting from the death of your friend."

"Allie wasn't my friend," said Isabelle casually. "And it's not like I'm the one that killed her. Do you blame the producers of *Planet Earth* when a gazelle gets mauled by a lion?"

"You had an innocent man arrested!" I said in disbelief. "He didn't give you that phone. He's going out of business because of your accusation."

"Gabriel?" she laughed. "The museum was already on its way out. He was never any good at adapting to the online era — that's the future of Lonesome Woods tourism."

"You ruined a man's life!" My voice got louder.

"Cost of doing business." She shrugged. "Why do you care what happens to that creep anyway?"

I gritted my teeth. "*He's not a creep*"

She raised her eyebrows and then smirked. "Oh… I see."

"What?"

"He's hot, I'll give you that," she said. "A bit out of your league though. And I'm not sure how the school would feel about you dating the curator of their *favorite* museum."

I clenched my fists.

"Tell you what…" She stood up. "I'll keep your little secret if you keep mine. We'll both just pretend like nothing happened. Deal?"

I wanted so badly to hit her — to knock that smug expression off her face. Jesus Christ, what was this place doing to me?

Before I could do something I would regret, I pointed to the door. "*OUT!*"

"Already on it, love." She stepped out of my office and blew me a kiss. "*Toodles.*"

I hurled a stapler at the closed door and had to stop myself from screaming. Gabriel was going to leave Lonesome Woods forever because of her — because of me.

Knock knock.

"What do you want?" I snapped.

But when the door creaked open, it wasn't Isabelle.

It was Oliver.

"Oh," I said sheepishly. "Sorry. Hi, Oliver. What's going on?"

Oliver bent down to pick up the stapler from the ground, and then he placed it on my desk.

"May I speak with you — in the professional sense?"

I raised my eyebrows. "Of course. Please. Close the door and take a seat."

He did as I asked and took a notebook out from his backpack.

"I believe I am having trouble processing Allie's death."

I leaned forward. "Tell me more, Oliver."

"I'm quite good at history, but I'm bad at math," he said. "Allie always helped me with algebra."

"Yes," I said gently. "She was a good, supportive friend."

"I was doing algebra homework this morning, and I believe I felt the emotion of sadness."

"What did that feel like?"

Oliver thought for a moment. "Heavy and perplexing. Like my heart went from a solid to liquid state."

"I understand," I said. "I felt that way too."

"You did?" Oliver brightened up. "So I am feeling sadness

correctly?"

I smiled encouragingly. "There's no right or wrong way to feel sadness. But what you've described is normal and healthy."

"Excellent," he said, relieved. "I've been told I'm 'emotionally retarded', so I wanted to confirm with you."

I shook my head. "Oliver, that's not true at all. You're sensitive and kind."

"Thank you for the feedback," he said, scribbling down some notes. "While I'm here, I would also like to discuss Wyatt."

"Okay," I said, straightening up. "What have you got for me?"

"I'm worried that Wyatt is also struggling," he said. "He drinks alcohol quite frequently — even during class."

I sighed. "Yes. I'm going to talk with him. I think he's having trouble with Allie's death too."

"I believe it to be more than that," said Oliver. "He appears to be experiencing emotions of shame and fear."

"Oh," I said, surprised. I hadn't noticed that. "I'll look into that."

"Thank you," said Oliver, as if he was working through a mental checklist of items. "The concern I feel for Wyatt has informed me that I may have developed feelings for him. I have written down a list of qualities I enjoy about Wyatt. He is funny. He is nice to me. He is humble. He asks me questions about the Civil War."

I gave him a smile. "I think he has feelings for you too, Oliver."

"Really?" He tilted his head. "But he has a girlfriend."

"Well, I don't think he likes her very much."

Yikes, that was wildly unprofessional and vindictive.

"Sorry," I said hurriedly. "Don't write that down. I would just keep up your friendship and see what happens."

"Thank you for the feedback," he said, flipping through the notebook. "I have one final item I would like to discuss."

I liked his down-to-business approach to counseling. "Go ahead."

"The word '*English*' written in chalk," he said. "I believe that could be a reference to Christopher English, the only remaining teacher from Timothy's time at Lonesome Woods. I enjoy his class very much."

Tingles ran up my spine. I remembered Gabriel telling me that one of Timothy's teachers was worried about him before he went missing. Christopher English was a history teacher, and Oliver was right — he was the only one still here from the era when Timothy disappeared.

"That's… That's a really good thought," I said. "I'll talk with him today."

Oliver nodded and put away his notebook. "Thank you. We have covered all the items I wished to address."

"Great," I said, standing up. "Oliver, I appreciate you coming in today. You're very thoughtful — and efficient."

Oliver nodded and put on his backpack.

"Thank you for the feedback."

Mai
I keep seeing Timothy in my dreams ever since coming here. How do I make it stop. The moment I close my eyes his face haunts me.

BASEBALL

"Christopher," I said, stepping into his classroom.

"Elliot," he said with a warm smile. "What a pleasant surprise. Please, come in."

It was easy to see why Oliver — and everyone else at the school — liked him. Christopher English was the epitome of a sweet old man. Heavyset with kind eyes and rosy cheeks, he reminded me of my grandfather.

"Can I make you some tea?" he asked, tending to an electric kettle on his desk.

"No, thank you," I said.

He nodded and brought over his own steaming mug, taking a seat at one of the desks with me.

"What can I help you with?" he asked.

"I've been looking into Allie Pruitt's death."

"Oh." He looked down sadly. "Yes, that poor girl."

"This might be a long shot," I said. "But that same evening, we found an unusual drawing on the Granite Footpath."

He raised his eyebrows. "A drawing?"

"Yes, in chalk," I said. "It's not the first one. A boy with red

58

hair — who I believe might be Timothy Small."

"Timothy Small…" He took a sip from his tea. "Now there's a name I haven't heard in quite some time."

"So you knew him?" I asked hopefully.

"Of course," he said. "Timothy was a wonderful student. Bright, motivated, clever. One of the best I've ever taught."

"Can you think of any reason why your name might have been written beneath the drawing of him?"

"*My* name?" His eyes went wide with a sudden… panic? But then he seemed to calm himself. "This would be the first I'm hearing of it."

"Well, it only said *English*. But I've run out of ideas, and I thought… maybe—"

"If you're searching for answers about Timothy's disappearance, I'm afraid I can't be of much help."

"Why not?" I asked.

Christopher bit his lip. "I'm forbidden from discussing it."

"Forbidden?" I said. "By who?"

He looked down.

"Christopher…" I said. "Kids are dying here. Whatever you tell me, I promise I won't share it with anyone."

He eyed me anxiously. "It'll be protected by that… doctor patient confidentiality thing?"

"Yes," I said. "I can draw up some paperwork if you'd like."

"No… That won't be necessary," he said. "But you must not repeat this to anyone — especially Henrik. If he finds out I'm talking about this again, I'll lose my job."

"You have my word," I said, growing more and more curious by the second.

He nodded. "Alright… Well, like I said, Timothy was a fantastic student. But he had a lot of trouble making friends. He was a funny looking kid — you know the awkward teenage years. So he spent a great deal of time with me during my office hours. Over the years, we talked about much more than his coursework. Most of it was lighthearted discussions about history and politics. But several weeks before his disappearance, he confided in me that he was a homosexual."

"Really?" I said. "I'd never heard that."

"That's because you're the third person to ever know about it."

"Third?" I said. "You, me, and…"

"His father, Henrik," said Christopher. "And Henrik did not take kindly to the news."

"How so?"

"You must understand, it was a different time," said Christopher. "Things like civil unions and same-sex marriage weren't even being discussed. Having a gay son was a mark of shame for many fathers, especially a military man like Henrik."

"So what, he disowned his son?"

"Worse, I'm afraid…" said Christopher sadly. "He nearly beat Timothy to death with a baseball bat — convinced he could smash the homosexuality from his body. The poor child was horrifically bruised for weeks."

"What?" I gasped. "I thought that came from bullies at the school?"

"He had plenty of those as well," said Christopher. "But the worst bully in his life was his father."

"So that's why he disappeared?" I asked. "To escape from Henrik?"

"Timothy didn't disappear…" Christopher put down his tea and blinked back tears. "He — he was murdered."

My blood went cold. "Why would you say that?"

But before he could answer, the door swung open and Henrik marched in.

"What are you doing here, Elliot?" he demanded.

"Oliver is having some trouble with history," I lied and stood up. "He's not formally diagnosed with a learning disability, but I was just suggesting Christopher give him some more time on his tests."

Christopher nodded and wiped his eyes. "Yes, I think it's a good idea."

Henrik eyed us suspiciously.

Fortunately, I managed to slip out the door before he could interrogate me further — or beat me with a baseball bat.

S+R♡ from South East
Thought it would be a good date night location as we love scary
stuff but upon arrival we got more than what we bargained for...
Words can't even describe... the nightmares still haven't
stopped I'm beginning to think they never will...

MOONLIGHT

Rain trickled down the tombstones as a bird crowed from the trees nearby.

I was back at the graveyard... alone in the middle of the night.

The coffin lay open in the grave by my feet... ready for my viewing.

I wanted to look inside, but I was frightened. I couldn't seem to remember what I had seen last time. All I knew was that it was too terrible for words.

I wished Gabriel was here with me. I felt safe and protected with him.

As if in answer to my thoughts, Gabriel glided out from the mist in the forest — covered only by a silver tulle cloak.

"You came back," I whispered, gazing at his body through the mesh material.

"Of course..." Gabriel stood by my side and held my hand. "I will always be here for you."

I swallowed and squeezed his hand.

"I'm — I'm scared to look inside the coffin."

Gabriel's eyes twinkled as he brushed a hand through my hair.

"I will help you, Elliot…"

He wrapped both of his arms around my shoulders and began to sway slowly back and forth, like waves in the ocean.

I closed my eyes and placed my hands on his bare waist, moving my body with his.

As we danced in the moonlight, his lips found their way to my neck. Like an animal playing with its food, he licked and sucked the area until it was tender.

I felt no pain as his teeth punctured the skin in my neck.

Only pleasure, as his body pressed closer to mine.

Then he pulled me down to the ground, holding me on top of him. Our heads were now just inches from the grave and coffin.

"*Look, Elliot…*" his voice commanded.

I writhed and brushed my face against his hair as he bit deeper.

"*Look…*"

I moaned and peered over his shoulder as he drank my blood.

I should have been horrified by what I saw in the coffin — but Gabriel had taken away my fear.

Inside, there was a severely bruised boy with bright red hair. His skin was a sickening mix of dark purples and jaundiced yellows. His face was so swollen that it was nearly unrecognizable. Two bloodshot eyes stuck out from the puffy mess, struggling to stay open against all the inflammation.

I knew those eyes.

Dash

Ten minutes without a guide. That's all it took. Lost, hungry, scared. Oh look! Cooked meat, a little old, a little burnt, but it's something. Something to keep away the insanity. Someone please help. Why does this school look familiar yet distant? Didn't there used to be a dorm there? Have I... been here? Did I ever leave? ...

SICK

The next day, I stopped by Christopher's classroom to learn more about Timothy's apparent murder. I had learned my lesson about jumping to conclusions and accusations without getting the full story first.

But when I peeked inside, I instead saw one of the substitute teachers preparing notes on the chalkboard. He was heavier set with blonde hair, light freckles and a beauty mark.

"Oh," I said, going pink. "Hey Will. Do you know where I might find Christopher?"

Will was the first gay man I'd met at Lonesome Woods, so naturally we had to try dating each other. He dumped me because I "seemed too desperate" — words that still poisoned my mind every time I passed him in the halls.

Now I understood why people said not to date your coworkers.

"Elliot…" he said with a forced smile. "Christopher is out sick. He should be back tomorrow."

I nodded politely, trying to mask the relentless pang of rejection.

"I'll check back tomorrow then."

"Wait," he called after me. "Elliot."

I braced myself and turned around. "Yes?"

"I just…" He looked down uncomfortably. "I just wanted to say, I hope we can go back to being friends."

"Definitely." I nodded, eager to end this conversation as quickly as possible.

"That thing I said… about you being desperate… I was just lashing out. I shouldn't have said it."

"It's really fine," I said, trying to sound calm as my heart constricted with an unshakeable sense of dread.

"You're a really good guy," he continued his well-prepared speech. "And I'm sure you'll find someone who appreciates all your… needs."

My heart squeezed harder — an intolerable sense of defectiveness flooding through my entire body.

"Right." I turned to leave. "I'm sorry for my neediness."

"Wait, that's not what I meant!"

I bolted out the door and could barely catch my breath from the horrible tightness in my chest.

I would check for Christopher tomorrow.

But when I came back the next day, Will was still there.

And the next day.

And the next.

Lily from Prescott
I can't tell who is real and who isn't anymore… all of the blood… the cackling laughter in the walls… every time I try to leave, something or someone keeps me here. To anyone reading this… leave immediately, and save yourself. I'm slowly going mad, and you will too…

PAINT

I finally turned to the only person who might have answers — the latest man to dump me.

"Elliot, do you always enter businesses with signs that say *Closed?*"

Gabriel was standing on a stepladder in the empty room, painting the walls white. I was starting to realize that neither dream Gabriel nor real-life Gabriel ever seemed to wear a shirt.

"Sorry," I said. "I'm not here to talk about us. I promise. I'm here because I've learned something new about Timothy's disappearance, and I was hoping you might have some thoughts."

He extended his arm to the ceiling and brushed the corner.

"Very well," he said, stepping down from the ladder. "What have you learned?"

I swallowed nervously as he approached me.

"You can't repeat this to anyone," I said. "But I talked with his old teacher, who claimed that the bruises came from his father beating him."

Gabriel thought for a moment. "Interesting."

"And that's not all," I said. "He also seemed convinced that Timothy was — that he was murdered."

Gabriel tilted his head.

"Interesting," he said again.

I looked at him, trying to keep my eyes on his face. "That's all you have to say...? *Interesting?*"

He raised his eyebrows. "Well... Aside from this teacher, there seems to be only one other person who was convinced of Timothy's death — so convinced that he held a funeral for the boy."

"You really think Henrik could do that?" I asked. "To his own son?"

"I don't know..." said Gabriel, bending over to dip his brush in a bucket of paint. "But it certainly would be a clever place to bury a body... In a grave that everyone thinks is empty."

I felt my heart beating faster, sensing my strange dreams merging paths with reality.

"There's only one way to find out," I said quietly. "Do you think we should...?"

Gabriel gave me a funny look and then realized I wasn't joking.

"Are you — are you serious, Elliot?"

"Sorry," I said, embarrassed. "No, of course not. It was just a joke."

He glared at me and then returned to painting.

"I wish I could be of more help. I hope you have a nice day."

"Wait," I said, coming up to his side. "Gabriel... I'm sorry."

He stopped painting for a moment and turned to me. "Sorry for what? Having me arrested for asking children to record violent incidents, or inviting me to dig up a grave?"

I cringed at myself. "Both."

"These bizarre assumptions have me wondering what you think of my character, Elliot."

"I'm sorry," I repeated. "What can I do to make it up to you? I don't want us to leave things off like this — not before you go."

He took a breath and then sighed. "Take a brush."

"Huh?"

"Help me paint the room," he said. 'Then all will be forgiven."

"Really?" I said hopefully as I grabbed a brush from the newspaper on the ground. "Okay."

"And lose the shirt," said Gabriel. "The ogling must be mutual."

I went red. "You noticed that?"

"You're not exactly subtle, Elliot…" He finally gave me a small smile. "Now, go on."

I bit my lip anxiously and then nodded. Gabriel watched intently as I unbuttoned my collared shirt and removed my undershirt.

Then I stepped next to him and we got started.

We spent the entire evening painting and talking until the golden sunlight in the windows turned to dark. He told me more about the Lonesome Woods book he was writing. Then I learned all about his parents in New York City, his sister in California, and their yearly summer reunions on the coast.

It was like the first date we never got to finish.

"What about you?" he asked. "Are you close with your family?"

I accidentally let out a laugh and Gabriel raised his eyebrows.

"Sorry," I said, stepping down from a ladder. "No. I would not say we're close."

Gabriel tilted his head. "What do you mean?"

"Well…" I began. "My father left when I was young. The last thing I ever heard him say was I'm a 'weird kid'. And then I spent most of my childhood taking care of my mom, who blamed me for his departure."

Gabriel looked at me with wide eyes.

"Sorry," I said again, feeling embarrassed for over-sharing. "That was too much information."

He stepped forward and placed his white-painted hand on my shoulder.

"I'm so sorry, Elliot."

"It's okay," I mumbled, encouraged by his gesture. "It was a long time ago."

"One summer, you'll have to come to the coast with my family!" he said enthusiastically.

"Inviting me on vacation?" I looked at him eagerly. "Does that mean I'm forgiven?"

He smiled and leaned in closer to me. "Almost."

I thought he was coming in for a kiss, but then he brushed a white streak of paint across my chest.

"*Now* you're forgiven."

"Hey!" I laughed and painted my brush across his chest too.

We both backed away from each other for a second, brushes raised as we stared at each other's painted torsos.

Then he dropped his brush and lunged toward me. I dropped mine too.

As we kissed, his body pressed against mine, smearing paint everywhere. It was the hottest thing I had ever experienced in my life. My past dates tended to fizzle out quickly because I was always waiting for the other guy to make the first move — but Gabriel had no trouble leading.

We made out for what felt like hours, holding each other tight with white-stained hands until the paint began to dry. Eventually, we slid against the wall and sat down next to each other.

"You should stay…" I said quietly.

Gabriel ran a hand through my hair. "I miss the city, Elliot."

"But I feel like we barely got any time together," I said. "I've never gotten to know someone like you."

He gave me a smile. "I feel the same way."

"Then stay," I pleaded.

"Why don't you come to New York?" He sat up. "I can assure you, there's an endless supply of people who need therapy."

I thought for a second and sighed. "I can't leave the kids. Not now — not until we figure this out."

He nodded. "I figured as much. You're a bit turbulent, but you do have a good heart, Elliot."

I put my head on his shoulder. "We'll just have to fit in an entire relationship before you go."

Gabriel blinked sadly and kissed me on the neck.

"I'm only here for a few more weeks," he said softly. "Are you content with knowing it's temporary? I don't want to hurt you…"

I knew he was referencing my father leaving, displaying empathy that only made me like him more. I swallowed and fought back the burning sensation in my eyes.

"I don't mind."

Lindsay from Memphis
If you're reading this then it means that after what feels like years trapped here, my message finally reached someone. Stay far far away from here. Tell my sister I love her. I am lost, forever I believe. Just run. RUN. I hear him coming. RUN

HURTING

"What is WRONG with you!"

I returned to the dormitory and heard Isabelle shouting from the bathroom.

"What's going on in here?"

I hurried into the bathroom to see everyone crowded around Wyatt, who had his head in the toilet. They looked up and stared at me.

"Why are you covered in paint...?" asked Kat.

"Helping a friend move," I said. "What's going on?"

"Wyatt took pills," said Isabelle in her fake accent. "Apparently alcohol wasn't enough for him."

"What pills?" I said urgently, pushing them aside.

"Alprazolam," said Oliver, holding up an orange prescription bottle. "He said he took eight of them."

I grabbed the bottle from Oliver and sighed with relief when I saw the dosage: 0.25mg

"I keep telling these idiots, we need to take him to the nurse," said Kat.

"No," I said firmly.

Kat raised her eyebrows. "Aren't you supposed to be a faculty member…?"

"They'll kick him out. The school has a zero tolerance policy for recreational drug use," I said. "He took 2mg of Xanax. He'll be fine with some rest and hydration."

"Interesting…" said Kat. "I always pegged daddy for a narc, but you just gained a few brownie points. Does this mean I can smoke weed in here?"

"No," I said. "I hate the smell of marijuana."

"And back to narc…" she muttered, walking away.

Wyatt retched in the toilet again and Isabelle cringed in disgust.

"Ugh," she said. "I don't have the stomach for this. I'm going for a walk. Ollie, be a dear and tend to him."

Oliver nodded seriously and saluted her. "I am at your service."

She gave him a rude look and left the room.

"Wyatt…" I settled down next to them." Something is clearly going on with you. Can you—"

"Excuse me." Oliver peered his head in front of mine. "But I have been tasked with tending to Wyatt, and I don't believe this is the right time to explore his troubled mental state. Would you be amenable to speaking with him in the morning?"

I raised my eyebrows. "Umm… Sure."

"Thanks, buddy." Wyatt gave Oliver a thumbs up from the toilet.

I stood up and left them alone in the bathroom, checking back every half hour to make sure they were doing okay. But Oliver was as good a caretaker as any adult, and I soon felt comfortable enough slipping into bed. The paint had dried on my body, and I wasn't going to get access to the shower any time soon.

As the night wore on, I heard the two of them make their way back into the bedroom.

Wyatt sounded a bit less comatose as Oliver helped him into bed.

"Thanks again, little buddy…" he said. "You can go to sleep

if you want."

"Absolutely not," said Oliver. "I will sit by the foot of your bed through the night."

"You really don't have to—"

"I will not let anything happen to you," said Oliver decisively. "You are my responsibility and you are my friend."

"Okay." Wyatt's voice broke. "Thanks."

"May I get you anything? A glass of water? A cold towel?"

Wyatt was quiet for a moment, and then I heard him say: "Could you tell me one of your favorite Civil War stories?"

"It would be an honor!" Oliver sounded very excited. "Now, this is a bit before the war occurred, but I will tell you the tale of my two heroes: William and Ellen Craft."

I closed my eyes and listened as Oliver dove into a story of two married slaves who used disguises and fake identities to escape captivity.

Something about his voice was so gentle and thoughtful that it was almost impossible to stay awake. Even Kat didn't seem to have any sarcastic comments about his story.

As I drifted off to sleep, I managed to peek my eyes open one last time.

Wyatt was sound asleep, and Oliver quietly finished his tale as he pulled a blanket over his friend's shoulders.

"I'm sorry you're hurting, Wyatt."

Elisha from Lonesome woods

Can't wait for tonight it's going to be so fun! Oh wait haven't I done this before? Never mind hang on what's he doing? Why does he have that knife? Oh no it's happening again! ......When are you coming home? It's cold down here you promised Can't wait for tonight it's going to be so much fun! Oh wait haven't I done this before? Never mind hang on what's he doing? Why does he have that k—

RUN

Every day I checked Christopher's classroom, and every day I found nothing but awkward encounters with Will.

But on the day of the third incident, I found something different.

Students were crowded around the door, chattering nervously.

"What's going on here?" I asked, pushing my way through them.

I tried to open the door but the handle was locked, so I peered through the small rectangular glass pane.

My jaw dropped when I saw what was inside.

Sitting in the classroom seats, I counted nineteen students — or at least, I assumed they were students. They were all wearing executioner's masks and black cloaks, so I had no idea who they were.

At the front of the classroom was a strange contraption. Wood scaffolding supported one large beam above. On the beam there were two pulleys about six feet apart, with a single piece of rope running between them. Hanging from the end of each the rope — a noose.

Below each noose, a stool.

"Someone go get Henrik." I turned around. "Tell him to call the police. Now."

A few students hurried off, and I turned my attention back to the room.

"Hey!" I called, banging on the window. "Someone let me in!"

The masked people did not move a muscle. They remained eerily silent in their seats. No chant, no rhyme, nothing.

Then three of them stood up from the front row.

One led the other two, who appeared to have their hands bound by more rope.

Like an executioner escorting prisoners to their death, the executioner guided them onto the stools as they whimpered and their hands shook uncontrollably.

Then the executioner removed their masks.

"*Jesus Christ…*" I whispered.

It was Isabelle and Christopher English.

Heart racing, I smashed my elbow into the glass pane but couldn't break it.

The executioner fastened the two connected nooses around each of their necks as they both sobbed side-by-side.

"A chair!" I yelled. "Someone get me a chair or a fire extinguisher."

I turned back and saw the executioner hand each of them a dumbbell. Isabelle's was much larger, to the point that her arms were shaking to hold onto it.

What the hell were the dumbbells for?

A student rushed forward to give me a fire extinguisher, which I hurled into the glass pane. It finally shattered after my third try.

I reached my hand through the small window, cutting my arm on shards of glass. But feeling around, I couldn't seem to find the other side of the door knob. They had removed it, and barricaded themselves in with bookshelves.

"Please stop!" I begged the masked students. "I know you have some sort of secret that you can't share with me, but I promise I can help."

None of them even acknowledged my presence.

I watched in horror as the executioner stood behind both of them and kicked away their stools.

"No!" I cried.

Isabelle and Christopher fell quickly, their necks strained to the side but not broken — yet.

They both dangled in the air, at the exact same height.

Given that Christopher was much heavier, he should have hit the ground already and pulled Isabelle up even further.

And that's when I realized what the dumbbells were for — either of them could let go of their weight to let the other survive.

"Fuck!" I cried. "Where is Henrik? Where are the police?"

Looking around frantically, I realize that neither of them would be here in time to save anyone. Isabelle and Christopher had at best a minute before they would both choke to death.

And so I made the most disgusting decision I've ever made in my life.

"Christopher…" I said miserably through the window. "You have to let go."

His eyes flickered with fear and he gasped for air. His head shook violently. "No!"

"Christopher…" I repeated, heart sinking. "She's a child."

He struggled and kicked as Isabelle made a terrible gargling sound. The heavy weight was slipping from her fingers.

"Christopher…" I said his name gently, over and over again. "You have to save her. She has a whole life left to live."

He closed his eyes, tears pouring down his face.

"Christopher…"

And then I saw it. His fingers quivered.

But before he let go, he choked:

"Elliot. The — the grave."

He dropped the weight on the ground, and his body soared

upward with a sickening crack as the rope tightened around his neck.

Isabelle fell to the ground in a heap, sobbing and screaming as she clutched the weight in her hands.

"What the hell is going on here!"

I ignored Henrik as I stumbled away from the door, suddenly taken by an overwhelming dizziness.

"Elliot!"

As he shouted my name, I broke into a sprint down the hallway — nearly falling over several times.

"ELLIOT!"

I ran faster.

I had to get away from him.

I had to get away from the students.

I had to get away from this godforsaken school.

Aleynia
Please let me out! This smoke is so thick. I'm choking and everything is burning. I want to go home. I miss my parents. I don't want to be stuck here forever. I'm so scared.

LEAVING

"What are you doing, daddy?"

I looked up from my suitcase, not in the mood for Kat's shenanigans. I had already spoke with Henrik and the police, I certainly did not need to top it all off with Kat's insults.

"I'm leaving."

She raised her eyebrows. "Odd time for a vacation, isn't it?"

"No, I'm quitting."

There was no point in sugarcoating it. They would all find out soon enough anyway.

She nodded and took a seat on my bed. "I heard what happened."

"Mhm." I grunted, returning to my packing.

She cracked her gum a few times, swinging her legs back and forth.

"You did the right thing, you know."

I stopped folding a shirt. "Sorry, Kat. I don't want to talk about it."

She sprawled back in my bed and stretched her arms above her head.

"I don't think you should leave."

"Well, sorry to disappoint—"

"I mean, who else at the school would have made that call?" she said. "You're the only reason another one of us didn't die today."

I dropped the shirt, heart racing. "I'm the reason a teacher died!"

"He was almost 80," said Kat. "It was like a fucked up version of the trolley problem, and you made the right call."

I shook my head. "Well, I can't do it anymore. This place won. Feels like I'm losing my mind. I barely sleep anymore — constant nightmares. And I still can't think of a single goddamn reason why more and more students are becoming infected with some sort of disease that turns them into brain-dead sociopaths."

"So that's it then?" said Kat. "You're just going to throw in the towel and abandon me here with the drunk and Ulysses S. Grant?"

I looked at her, exasperated. "What do you want from me, Kat?"

"I already told you," she said. "I want you to stay."

"Why?" I asked. "You've never seemed particularly fond of me."

She averted her eyes and cracked her gum a few more times. "Because — Because I feel safe with you."

I raised my eyebrows and felt my heart soften. "You do?"

She rolled over and glared at me. "Breathe a word of that to anyone and you're dead, daddy."

"That's more like it…" I finally managed a small smile.

But before I could think much more about Kat's words, Isabelle stepped through the door.

"Elliot…" she said meekly.

"Isabelle," I said, standing up. "How are you doing?"

"I'm okay," she said, eyes red. "Just here to pack my things."

"You're leaving?"

"Yes." She sniffed and wiped her nose. "I've been expelled. Please tell Wyatt we're finished. I hope he gets well soon."

"What? *Expelled?*" I didn't like Isabelle, but that seemed like a harsh punishment for a girl who had just survived a public hanging.

"Yes," she said again. "Henrik wants me gone by evening."

"What the hell?" I screwed up my face. "That's insane. I'll talk to him."

"I already did." She walked over to her bureau. "I told him everything. About the blog. About the camera. About how I made up the stuff with Gabriel."

"Whaaaat?" Kat sat up.

"Oh." I bit my lip and stepped up behind Isabelle. "You didn't have to do that, Isabelle."

She started yanking out the clothes from her drawers.

"Isabelle?"

She pulled the clothes out faster and faster, hurling them into a pile on the floor.

"*Isabelle?*"

She finally stopped and turned around, cheeks stained with tears.

Then she pulled me into a tight hug and began to sob uncontrollably.

"Thank you," she choked. "Thank you. Thank you. Thank you."

Sean from Cambridge
It feels like I am losing more and more of myself each day.

RAFAEL

If I was going to stay at this school, I would need something to ground me.

"Elliot!" Gabriel hurried over to me and gave me a kiss. My heart soared as his soft lips seemed to wipe away the day's events.

"Are you okay?" He gently ran a finger below my eye. "You look as if you've been crying."

"Yeah," I said. "It was just — it was a rough day."

"I'm sorry to hear that," he said. "Perhaps this will cheer you up."

He grabbed my hand and brought me to the corner of the empty room, where I saw a picnic blanket and an incredible spread of food.

I smiled. "What is this, Gabriel?"

"Grapes, shrimp cocktail, cheese, crackers, strawberries, chocolate... and a full pitcher of water, of course."

I laughed and kissed him. "You made us a picnic — I love it."

We sat down across from each other and dove into the food. This was exactly what I needed to take my mind off of things.

We chatted and laughed for hours, never seeming to run out of spiritual or psychological discussions. I felt like I could talk with him forever.

Gabriel gazed into my eyes. "Why did you decide to become a therapist?"

"Oh." I raised my eyebrows and thought for a moment. "Well, I guess… I struggled with a lot with my sexuality, being raised religious and all."

"Struggled how?" asked Gabriel.

"I…" I had never told anyone this aside from my childhood therapist, but something about Gabriel just made me open up. "I have scars. I self-harmed — down there."

Gabriel reached out to hold my hand. "I'm sorry, Elliot."

"It's okay," I said. "It was a long time ago. And I guess some part of me always felt my dad left because of me — because there was something wrong or defective about me."

Gabriel tilted his head. "You formed a false conclusion about yourself, based on the actions of a trusted loved one."

"Exactly," I said. "It was such a persistent, nagging doubt about myself. My childhood therapist helped me through it. And she inspired me to make sure nobody else went through something like that alone."

Gabriel thought for a moment. "Do you know the meaning of my name?"

"Gabriel?" I said, confused by the sudden change in topic. "One of the seven archangels — God's messenger."

"Precisely," said Gabriel, holding his hand to my heart. "And I am here to deliver a message to you… That you were created with great intention, Elliot. That you are perfect and whole, exactly as you are."

My heart softened further.

"You are here to help the world…" Gabriel continued. "Because another of the archangels lives in your heart… The angel of healing."

He brushed a hand through my hair and whispered into my neck, "*Rafael…*"

Tingles and light surged through my body as he kissed my

neck and unbuttoned my shirt.

"But even the angel of healing can become wounded."

His warm breath on my chest was like nothing I had ever known.

"Let me heal your scars, Rafael…"

My heart melted as Gabriel's lips moved further and further down my body.

> Amiya
> *What happened to me ? I entered the building and I felt like a*
> *fell through a portal...*

FRAUDS

I returned to the dormitory by curfew with a new lease on life.

"Hello Kat!" I said, practically dancing into the room. "Oliver! Wyatt!

"Wow..." Kat glanced up from her book. "Someone's in a better mood. You get laid or something?"

"What!" I sputtered, quickly spiraling back down to reality. "No — No, I just went for a good long walk and cleared my mind."

"Right," said Kat with a smirk. "Glad you're feeling better, daddy. Does this mean you'll be staying?"

"Yes," I said. "I'm staying."

"I'm glad to hear that." Oliver walked up to me. "Because in your absence, I patrolled the Granite Footpath, and another drawing has appeared near the tennis courts."

My heart sank. I had completely forgotten that drawings came after each incident.

"What did this one say?" I asked nervously.

"Well," said Oliver, flipping through his notepad. "It had the same red-haired stick figure, but this time the message said: *FRAUDS*."

He looked up at me, as if expecting me to explain what that meant.

"I suppose it makes sense for Isabelle," I said, trying to think. "She was—"

"A fake-ass bitch?" Wyatt slurred from his bed. "That's right. Kat told me everything."

"Wyatt, are you using again?"

"So what if I am?" he said defensively. "I just found out I got dumped by my pathologically lying girlfriend."

I sighed. I didn't have time to take care of Wyatt tonight.

"Oliver, can you…"

"I'm already on it." He nodded seriously and saluted me.

I felt bad assigning a student to do my job, but I had something important to do.

After Henrik's repeated mind-lapses, I had done something very bad — something that could undoubtedly get me kicked out of the school.

I had installed cameras on the Granite Footpath.

Kaylan
Where are we? I don't even remember the ride here.

MOVEMENT

My hands shook as I sat in my dark office, face illuminated only by the computer screen.

Scrolling through hours of video, I still had no idea what was causing the students to behave this way, but I had a feeling I was about to discover *who* was behind it all.

And I was pretty sure I knew who it was.

Henrik was the only person I had told about Isabelle being a sightseer, and he had also walked in on me talking with Christopher English the day before Christopher went out "sick".

It didn't make any logical sense though. Henrik was not some kind of psychopath. He was not calm, he was not calculated, and he was certainly not have shallow affect.

If anything, Henrik was the opposite of those things. He was neurotic. Unstable. Delusional, even.

So why would he spend his entire life waging a war against an imaginary curse, while simultaneously harming the students he was obsessed with protecting?

I didn't want to dig up that grave, so I was hoping to get the answers I needed from this video.

But as the night wore on, the footage never changed. Just an empty, untraveled path in greyscale. I would have thought I was staring at an extremely boring image, if not for the occasional drops of rain that obscured the view.

I was about to call it a night and resume my search in the morning when I finally saw it.

Movement.

My heart raced as I watched the figure appear from the south side of the screen, making their way to exactly where the drawing was found.

I leaned in close to the screen and watched as the figure bent down, produced a piece of chalk from their pocket, and began to scribble.

I zoomed in.

"*Come on…*" I whispered. "*Look up, Henrik…*"

But the figure remained hunched over as they finished the drawing, and then stood up with their face turned away from the camera.

They were about to walk off the screen, but then they turned around once — flashing a blurry face.

"*Yes…*" I muttered, zooming in. "*Gotcha.*"

But as the updated picture rendered on my screen, my heart sank.

That wasn't Henrik.

It wasn't even an adult.

It was Wyatt.

Katie from Stockport
Help, it's dark and I can't get out!

TRAPPED

"I need all of you to leave."

"Ummm…" Kat rolled over. "In case you've forgotten, we live here."

I pointed to the door. "Out. Now."

She raised her eyebrows and jumped down from the bed. "*Daddy's in a mood…*"

"But you tasked me with caring for Wyatt," said Oliver.

"I'll be taking the next shift now," I said. "Thanks for your help."

Oliver nodded and followed Kat out of the room.

Wyatt tried to sit up and stumble out of bed, but I pushed him back.

"Not you. You're staying."

"What…?" he said groggily. "What's going on, Elliot?"

I handed him a large cup of water.

"Drink."

He gave me a weird look and took a sip.

"All of it. Chug it."

"Elliot…"

"CHUG IT."

I knew he was high, but I didn't care. After Isabelle, I couldn't handle more betrayal and lies.

His eyes went wide and he did as I said, spilling water all over the bed.

"Why did you do it, Wyatt?" I asked, at a loss. "Are you a sightseer too?"

He put the water glass down. "I honestly don't know what you're talking—"

"STOP LYING TO ME!" I shouted. "I SAW YOU MAKE THE DRAWING."

His expression sank and he shrank back into bed.

"No…" he moaned. "No you didn't."

"Tell me why you did it, Wyatt!" I said desperately. "Why the hell are you drawing these things, Wyatt?"

"No…" He shook his head and pulled a pillow over his head. "Leave me alone."

I grabbed the pillow and threw it aside. "Enough! Talk now, or I'll take you to the police."

He looked at me miserably, eyes watering. "Please, Elliot… Don't make me."

I took a deep breath and realized my shouting wasn't helping anything.

"Wyatt…" I said gently. "I understand you are hurting. Allie was hurting too. And it's my job to help you. I promise, no matter what you're going through, I can make it better."

"No, you can't," he choked. "Not this."

"Can you at least give me a chance to try?" I asked. "You know me, Wyatt. You know I'm going to do everything in my power to help you."

"You don't understand," he said. "I'm — I'm trapped."

I leaned closer to him, and put my hand on his quivering shoulder.

"Then let me free you."

He looked up at me, broken.

And then finally — a nod.

"Please don't tell anyone…" he whispered. "Please, Elliot. I'm begging you."

"I won't," I said. "You have my word."

He swallowed, closed his eyes, and stumbled up from the bed.

"Where are you…"

But I decided to shut up as he dug through his bureau drawers and returned to me with a cell phone.

Jesus, the black market at this school was worse than prison.

He unlocked the phone and handed it to me, arms shaking.

Then he crawled back into bed and buried his face in the blankets.

I looked at the screen curiously and began to read through Wyatt's private social media messages.

Within a few seconds, my blood went cold.

Within a few minutes, I was horrified.

Finally, it all made sense — a real, psychological explanation for every single incident.

And it was infinitely scarier than any curse.

> Daria
> *Who are you? And what am I doing here? What is this place?*
> *And why is it so cold...?*

ATTACHED

Kristie P:
Hey Wyatt! I saw your profile. I'm a scout for a modeling agency, and I think you'd make a great fit for our brand.

Me:
Really? Haha

Kristie P:
Definitely! You have the exact look we're going for. We pay $10,000 per photo.

Me:
Damn… Ok. I'm in.

Kristie P:
Awesome! To start, can you send me a couple of head

shots so I can take them back to my manager for approval? They don't need to be anything professional. Selfies are fine.

Me:
Sure.

Me:
<IMAGE ATTACHED>
<IMAGE ATTACHED>
<IMAGE ATTACHED>

Kristie P:
Great! I'll let you know what my manager says.

Kristie P:
Good news! He loved them. I've attached our contract for your approval. As discussed, the rate is $10,000 per photo. If you're interested, could you please sign and scan it back to me? Thanks Wyatt!
<DOCUMENT ATTACHED>

Me:
<DOCUMENT ATTACHED>

Kristie P:
Perfect!

Kristie P:
Alright, Wyatt. Everything is all set on our end. To get an idea of your body type, could you send along a

couple of shirtless photos?

Me:
Haha ok.

Me:
<IMAGE ATTACHED>
<IMAGE ATTACHED>

Kristie P:
These are great. I'm thinking of putting you in our A-tier group. This is our most exclusive group, and you'd be offered the best opportunities. I'll need to check with my manager first.

Me:
Wow cool haha

Kristie P:
Hello Wyatt! Hope you had a nice week. More good news! My manager is interested in putting you in the A-tier group. To move forward with that, could you please send along a few full frontal photos? These won't be used in any materials. It's simply to determine how your body will fit into various clothing and underwear lines.

Me:
Like naked?

Kristie P:
Yes, if you're comfortable with that. If not, I'm happy to

put you in a lower tier where we won't need that. But I cannot promise you'll receive the same modeling opportunities.

Me:
No it's alright. Just wanted to check

Me:
And these won't be used in anything public?

Kristie P:
That's correct, Wyatt!

Me:
<IMAGE ATTACHED>
<IMAGE ATTACHED>
<IMAGE ATTACHED>

Kristie P:
Perfect! I'll get these back to my manager and let you know about the A-tier group.

Me:
Ok thanks

Me:
Hey, did you hear anything about the group?

Me:
Hey, just checking in again?

Me:
Hey, sorry. I'm sort of freaking out about those pictures. Could you delete them? I don't think I want to do the modeling thing anymore.

Kristie P:
Wyatt. If you tell anyone about the conversation we're about to have, I will forward your photos to all of your friends and family.
<IMAGE ATTACHED>
<IMAGE ATTACHED>
<IMAGE ATTACHED>

Me:
What? I won't. I promise.

Kristie P:
Tomorrow afternoon there will be an incident in your lunchroom. Later that evening, you will walk the Granite Footpath. You will find chalk beneath the Weeping Willow tree. You will draw a picture on the path. It will look like this.
<IMAGE ATTACHED>

Me:
What are you talking about? Who is this?

Kristie P:
Yes or no, Wyatt? Remember I have these.
<IMAGE ATTACHED>
<IMAGE ATTACHED>

<IMAGE ATTACHED>

Me:
Yes.

Me:
I did it. Please delete the pictures.

Me:
Hello?

Kristie P:
It's time for another drawing, Wyatt. Just like the last one, but tonight the message below must say SEVEN.

Me:
Why?

Kristie P:
Do not question me. Additionally, you will shout the number SEVEN when on the third chant of "PICK A NUMBER"

Me:
What? What does that mean?

Kristie P:
You'll understand shortly.

Me:
You made me kill my friend

Me:
Fuck you EVIL bitchh!!!

Kristie P:
Knock it off or I will send these to your mom and dad.
<IMAGE ATTACHED>
<IMAGE ATTACHED>
<IMAGE ATTACHED>

Me:
Sorry I was drunk. It won't happen again.

Me:
Sorry. Please don't send them.

Kristie P:
It's time for the next drawing, Wyatt. Tonight's message will read FRAUDS.

Me:
Ok

Squeak

I haven't seen another living person since arrival.. what is this place? They said it was haunted, but I never believed in ghosts.. I was so wrong, please forgive me.

MONSTROUS

I looked up from the phone in shock.

This was disgusting. This was monstrous. This was evil.

But it finally made sense how this "curse" was spreading.

"Wyatt…" I said quietly, pulling the covers from his head.

"Don't look at me," he cried and buried his face in his arms.

"Wyatt…" I repeated. "You have nothing to be ashamed of."

"Did you — did you even read it?"

"Yes," I said gently. "You didn't do anything wrong."

"I'm the reason Allie jumped!" His voice got louder.

"No, you aren't…" I said. "Allie felt forced to jump. She was very likely being threatened with the same situation as you."

"What?" He looked up at me. "What do you mean?"

"All of these incidents," I said. "The students stabbing themselves with forks, standing on the wall, staging an execution… None of them *wanted* to be doing that."

He wiped his eyes. "You think Kristie got to them too?"

"Yes," I said. "And none of you have anything to be

ashamed of. You've been victimized by a predator."

"But she can ruin our lives," he said. "We'll never go to college or get a job."

"Yes you will," I said. "We're going to put an end to this."

"You can't tell anyone!" said Wyatt. "You promised."

I nodded. "I know. But there are other ways to navigate this."

"Like what?"

"First, I need you to tell me where you got this phone. How did you get it past security?"

"I didn't," he said simply. "I found it under my covers a few weeks before all this started. It didn't even have a passcode. I thought I had hit the jackpot."

"Can I have the phone?"

His eyes went wide. "No. What if I miss one of her demands?"

"It will only be for a little while," I promised. "If you receive any threats, I'll be sure to tell you right away."

He hesitated for a second and nodded. "Okay."

"Good," I said, pocketing the phone. "Last question. Do you have any idea when the next incident will be?"

"No." He shook his head. "She only ever messages me the morning it happens."

"Got it," I said, standing up. "I'm going to go get the others to look after you while I take care of a few things. I promise I'll be back shortly."

"Elliot…" he said faintly.

I turned around. "Yes?"

"Please don't tell Oliver."

"Of course not," I said. "But… Wyatt, you might try confiding in your friends so you don't have to go through this alone. I think you'll find that Oliver is not exactly the judgmental type. I think he… cares for you."

"Really?" asked Wyatt hopefully.

"Definitely," I said with a smile. "So let him help you. He has a really good heart."

Wyatt wiped his eyes and laid back into bed.

"Yeah, he does."

> Teigan from Ipswich
> *This is weird. Where am I? This can't be happening. I have to get home*

PROMISE

"Elliot, you look unusually awful."

"Thanks," I said, taking a seat across from my best friend at our usual tea spot. "Sorry I'm late. Traffic on the highway was bad."

"I ordered your usual," said Zach, pushing a cup to me.

"Thanks," I said again, taking a quick sip. I wanted to get past the formalities and get straight to business.

"Everything okay?" he asked. "Still broken up about Will?"

"What?" I scoffed. "What are you talking about?"

He raised his eyebrows. "The last time I saw you, you were nearly in tears about what he said — the thing about you being too desperate."

"I was not in *tears*!" I said defensively. "God, Zach. I'm fine."

"Oh, good," he said. "Because for a while there it sounded like you were never going to date again."

"Well if you must know, I actually *am* seeing someone."

Zach looked up from his tea with a smile. "Oh?"

"Yes," I said. I didn't have time for this right now.

Zach gave me an annoying smile. "Care to elaborate...?"

I sighed and gave him the SparkNotes. "His name is Gabriel.

He runs a museum near the school. I really like him. We have a lot of interesting conversations."

"That's great!" said Zach, like a dad encouraging his child. "So where do you see things going with this Gabriel guy?"

"Nowhere," I said, biting my lip. "He's leaving soon. Moving to New York."

Zach tilted his head. "Elliot... What are you doing?"

"What do you mean?"

Zach sighed. "Are you really going to make me say it?"

"Well, it doesn't sound like I'm going to stop you. So go ahead."

Zach looked into my eyes. "Why do you keep going after men who are unavailable?"

"I do not!"

"Really?" said Zach, holding up his fingers to start counting. "Let's start with us—"

"Oh my god." I rolled my eyes. He was referring to an unreciprocated crush I once had on him when we were kids. "I know you think you destroyed all other men for me—"

"I'm not the one who did that."

"Excuse me?"

I could tell Zach was afraid of what he was about to say, but he said it anyway.

"Elliot, you're a therapist!" he said, exasperated. "Can't you see that you're just re-living your father's rejection, over and over again?"

"Ridiculous—"

"Is it?" he asked. "Because it feels like every time you do this, you end up devastated and wondering why you're not enough — which is exactly the Elliot I remember from long ago."

"You're completely incorrect."

Zach reached across the table to touch my hands. "I just... I don't want to see you hurt."

"Well, this has been fun." I pulled my hands away. "But I actually have something I need to ask you."

He opened his mouth to continue arguing, but then stopped himself.

"Alright," he said. "What do you need?"

I dug into my pocket and put Wyatt's phone on the table.

"Can you do your journalism investigation thing with this?"

"My… journalism investigation thing…?"

"I read every one of your articles," I said. "Sometimes you say you 'traced' calls or texts or emails back to the sender."

"I mean, I do have some contacts that help me—"

"Perfect," I said, opening up Wyatt's social media messages. "I need you to figure out who this Kristie P profile is."

I handed him the phone and watched as he began scrolling.

"Elliot…" he whispered. "What have you gotten yourself into?"

"Oh, and heads up — there are some nude photos of a student coming."

"God!" He shoved the phone back at me. "What is *wrong* with you?"

"He's eighteen."

"Oh, well in that case, please let me continue."

I nodded and pushed the phone back to him.

He stared at me, jaw dropped. "I was being sarcastic."

"Zach, come on!" I pleaded. "Someone is exploiting kids at this school. This is just one of potentially dozens. I need to figure out who's doing this to them, so they can feel safe coming forward."

"Why don't you go to the police? Or the school?"

"I will," I said. "But right now, I'm worried the headmaster could be involved. So I brought this to the only person I know I can trust."

Zach sighed and shook his head. "This is so bad, Elliot."

"Does that mean you'll do it?" I asked eagerly.

He thought for a moment. And then to my tremendous relief, he grabbed the phone and shoved it in his pocket.

"Promise me you will *never* involve me in something like this again."

I took a sip from my tea.

"I promise."

Cameron from Gold Coast
Where am I?

ARCHANGELS

"It is time, Rafael…"

Gabriel and I stood together in the graveyard, holding hands as the rain trickled down our unclothed bodies.

"I'm not ready," I said, squeezing his hand. "I'm frightened."

"You have nothing to fear…" Gabriel pulled our bodies together. "I am here with you, Rafael."

I closed my eyes and embraced him, feeling every part of his naked body against mine — the slight movements of his chest and abs as he breathed.

"Let me calm you, Rafael…"

He turned me around, embracing me from behind. His glistening arms wrapped around my chest and inner thigh.

I let out a soft moan as he began to kiss my neck.

"Relax, Rafael…"

I relaxed as his teeth sunk into my neck.

"Are you ready, Rafael…?"

I moaned again and nodded.

I quivered as he entered my body, and the two archangels finally became one.

We made love under the stars, surrounded by the dead and forgotten.

Gabriel's lips alternated between my neck and my mouth, filling an endless hunger as he consumed every part of me.

Then, without warning, he pushed me into the grave.

"Gabriel!" I cried out, falling into the coffin with a thud.

Gabriel stepped forward and stood there — a towering shadow above me.

"It is time to look, Rafael…"

He began shoveling dirt on top of me.

"No!"

The dirt started to pile up on my bare skin.

"*Look, Rafael…*"

I winced and prepared to finally face my fear.

"*Look…*"

Turning slowly to my side, I saw the bruised boy laying next to me.

But he was not dead. Through black eyes and split lips, he stared at me sadly.

I knew those eyes….

Who was that?

As dirt filled the coffin all around us, I desperately brushed it away from his face — trying to keep him alive. But I was no match for Gabriel.

So together, the boy and I suffocated as dirt and worms filled our lungs.

"WAKE UP, ELLIOT!"

Kelsey from Belton
H-How did I get here? Somebody, please help! It's dark in here and I can't move for the ropes binding me!

DISGUSTING

"What! Huh?"

"Fuck, Elliot!" Kat was shaking me, and she was crying. "Wake the fuck up."

I rubbed my eyes and sat up from bed. What was happening?

"Look!" She pointed to the middle of the room.

I turned my head and saw something so bizarre that I had to wonder if I was still dreaming.

There were twenty — no, twenty-five — students standing in a circle in our room.

And in the center of the circle...

"OLIVER!" Wyatt cried out from his bed.

One of the students rushed up to Wyatt with a knife.

"Leave him alone!" begged Wyatt. "Please, put me there instead."

The student pushed the knife against Wyatt's throat, and he stopped talking.

"What the hell is going on here?" I demanded, finally waking up. "Get away from Oliver."

The knife-wielder approached me and held a finger to his

lips.

"*Shhh…*"

"I won't—"

He brought the knife to my neck and I felt blood start to drip down my skin. I swallowed and put my hands in the air. "Sorry." I breathed. "I'll stop."

He returned to the circle, and the students — many of whom I recognized from the previous incidents — began their next chant.

"*No son of mine…*"

One of them stepped to the center of the circle with a baseball bat. Oliver looked absolutely terrified and helpless.

"*Be gone, disgusting sickness…*"

Then the student smashed Oliver in the face with a baseball bat.

"NO!" Wyatt, Kat, and I screamed at the same time.

But every time we tried to intervene, we were shoved back into our beds and threatened with a knife.

"*No son of mine…*"

The next student stepped forward with the bat.

"*Be gone, disgusting sickness…*"

Oliver cried out in pain as the bat cracked against his skull.

"Do something, Elliot!" Wyatt sobbed. "Fuck!"

My mind was racing, trying to come up with a solution that didn't involve anyone getting stabbed or beaten.

"*No son of mine…*"

The next student came forward.

"*Be gone, disgusting sickness…*"

Kneecap shattered.

"*No son of mine…*"

"STOP!" I screamed.

"*Be gone, disgusting sickness…*"

The next student raised her bat. I knew her. She sat at our lunch table once a few months ago.

"QUINN!" I shouted desperately. "I KNOW ABOUT THE PHOTOS!"

She paused, holding the bat above her head.

The knife-wielder marched up to me, but I continued anyway.

"I know about all of your photos," I said, looking around the room. "And I know that you're terrified. But you need to understand that I'm going to help you."

Quinn slowly started to lower the bat.

"Help us how?" she asked, eyes welling with tears. "What can you do to stop it?"

This was not at all how I wanted to approach this. Rather than intimate one-on-one conversations like I had planned, I was now trying to treat twenty-five traumatized students at once.

"I know that you feel like your lives are over," I said. "Like you'll never go to college or find a job. Like everyone in your life will look at you in disgust."

"They will!" cried Quinn.

"No," I said gently. "This is a small blip in the grand scheme of things. Trust me. When I was your age, I did way more embarrassing things. And that was by choice — not by threat."

"What if you're wrong!" said another from the circle. "What if the pictures come out?"

"Then I'll help you," I said confidently. "Shame is an internal emotion. It does not have to stay with you any longer than you allow it to. You have all been victimized. You do not need to be ashamed of that. You need to put the shame back on the abuser, where it belongs."

I noticed Wyatt was listening to my every word intently.

"Please," I said to Quinn. "Put down the bat so we can fix this together."

She sniffled and finally dropped the bat.

I let out a huge sigh of relief, but then another student ran forward to grab the bat.

"We have to finish!" He stepped toward Oliver's already-contorted body. "The message said we all have to hit him — twenty-five times total. I have to send a picture as proof, or else they'll release our pictures."

"What's your name?" I asked calmly, standing up with my hands in the air. The knife-wielder wasn't even trying to stop me

106

anymore.

"B — Brett," he stammered.

"Brett, we're going to send them proof, okay?" I turned to Kat. "Kat, can you go grab your makeup?"

Without question, she ran to the bathroom.

The others looked at me in confusion as Kat and I pushed through the circle and approached Oliver.

"He already looks pretty messed up," I whispered to Kat. "Can you make him look worse?"

She swallowed and nodded. "Definitely."

Oliver whimpered as she started smudging his face, arms, and legs with her favorite black, purple, and blue makeup.

"Sorry, Ollie…" She blinked back tears and held his hand. "It won't be much longer."

When she was finished, she stepped away and I had to stop myself from gasping in horror. Oliver looked a lot like the bruised boy from my dreams — broken and barely recognizable.

"Brett, I'm assuming you have a phone to take the proof photo?"

He nodded and pulled it out of his pocket. "Yeah. Here."

"Just another minute, Oliver…" I promised, leaning closer to snap a few pictures. "And we're done."

"Wyatt and Kat, I want you to wash off the makeup and take Oliver to the nurse, okay?" I said. "If they ask, you tell them another incident has occurred. Be sure to tell them he was hit twenty-five times."

They nodded and helped Oliver up.

"For the rest of you," I said, turning to the students. "I need you to keep up the act a little longer, okay? If anyone asks, tell them you can't remember what happened tonight — just like the other incidents. And please come to me immediately if you receive messages about another incident."

"You're — you're not going to turn us in?" Quinn asked.

"Turn you in for what?" I asked, grabbing my bag. "You were thrown into an impossible situation, and you did what you thought you had to do to survive."

I threw the bag over my shoulder and made my way to the

door.

"What are you going to do now?" asked Brett.

I turned around to face twenty-five broken students — students who had been tormented and manipulated by a stranger for months.

They deserved some honesty.

"I'm going to dig up a grave."

Ellie Jayne from London
Help...please...someone??

SHADOW

I stepped out of my car, looking around the moonlit graveyard that had been haunting my dreams.

But there was no Gabriel tonight.

Just me — and a shovel.

There was no time to waste. I got to work quickly, driving the spade into the dirt and moss in front of Timothy's grave.

I knew it was illegal, but *everything* was pointing to this grave — my nightmares, Christopher English's last words, even Henrik himself had taken me here.

Hours disappeared into the night as piles of dirt around the grave grew larger and larger. It was significantly more difficult than I expected. And without Gabriel, it definitely lacked a certain... excitement.

I wasn't exactly sure what I was looking for, but I was surprised when I felt the *thud* of my shovel hitting wood — in what was supposed to be an empty grave.

"*What the...*"

I jumped down into the hole and my heart raced as I began

pushing aside more and more dirt to reveal the lid of a coffin.

I maneuvered myself into an awkward position and yanked at the top.

It took a few hard tugs, but eventually it opened.

"*Ugh…*" I coughed as dust filled my lungs.

As the cloud of debris dissipated, I looked closer and my heart sank.

Inside the coffin, I saw two things:

A skeleton, about the size of a young teenager.

And a baseball bat — that appeared to be stained with some sort of brown or black substance.

Ring! Ring!

"Jesus!"

I nearly had a heart attack as my cell phone rang and buzzed from my pocket.

I dug my hands into my pocket and fumbled with the phone. "Hello?"

"Elliot, it's Zach."

"Oh," I said. "Yeah. Hi."

"Is everything okay?" he asked. "You sound out of breath."

"Just went for a run," I said.

"At 4am…" asked Zach. "Where are you? Your connection is awful."

"Welcome to Lonesome Woods," I said. "Why are you awake now anyway?"

"I think I figured out your mysterious Kristie P."

My whole body lit up. "Really?"

"Yes," he said. "I sent her a message from another fake profile. I masked it to look like a photo from another student, but it was actually a link to my own server — and she clicked it."

"I don't get it."

"Well, once she clicked the link, I was able to obtain her IP address."

"Zach, I have no idea what you're saying," I said. "Who is it?"

"I looked up the IP address, and it's part of your school

network," he said. "It matches the same IP address found in archived email headers of various school communications."

"Zach, just tell me who it is!"

"It's… It's coming from the office of the headmaster."

My body went cold.

"What? Are you sure?"

"Someone named Henrik Small," he said. "Does that ring any bells?"

Before I could answer, headlights shone through the darkness above me.

Someone else was at the graveyard.

"*Elliot?*" Zach's voice came from the phone.

A car door opened and closed.

"Zach, call the police," I whispered into the phone. "I'm at the Lonesome Woods Cemetery."

Then I shoved the phone back into my pocket without hanging up.

"*Elliot? Hello?*"

I tried to pull myself up the side of the hole, but the dirt just crumbled from my fingers and I fell back into the grave.

A shadow appeared above me, and I looked up.

"Henrik."

Hannah from Wiltshire
Where am I? and how did I get here??

FATHER

"What the hell are you doing?" Henrik called down to me.

I could not think of a single believable excuse, so I decided to tell him the truth.

"Christopher… Christopher English told me to check the grave," I said. "Before he died."

"So you dig up my son's grave?!" His voice got louder.

"I'm sorry," I said. "But Henrik… There's a body in here."

Even from down here, I saw Henrik's face go pale.

"Nonsense."

"Look for yourself," I said. "There's also a baseball bat."

"The grave is empty!" he roared. "You put those things there."

"I didn't, Henrik…" I said. "But I know about how you used to beat your son. And there seems to be blood all over this bat."

"You're lying!" shouted Henrik. "You're — you're trying to frame me!"

"No," I said. "Your son was gay, and you thought you could beat it out of him."

"MY SON WAS NO FAGGOT!" Henrik roared into the

night.

I ignored him and continued. "Perhaps, one day… You took it too far?"

"I DIDN'T KILL TIMOTHY!" he screamed. "IT WAS — IT WAS THE CURSE — THE FUCKING RAIN."

"There is no curse, Henrik…" I said, shaking my head. "Someone has been manipulating the students to do these things… And I think it's been going on for years."

"ENOUGH, ELLIOT!"

"I know about your blackouts," I said, becoming increasingly aware that I was attempting to conduct a therapy session from a coffin. "I know strange things happen that you can't seem to remember."

"SHUT UP, OR I WILL BURY YOU ALIVE."

I took a deep breath. I didn't doubt his threat, but I had to continue. I had no other choice.

"Henrik, do you know what dissociation is?"

"DIS-WHAT?"

"Dissociation," I repeated. "It's a disconnect between your thoughts, memories, and identity. It is very often caused by psychological trauma."

"WHAT DOES THAT HAVE TO DO WITH ANYTHING?"

"Henrik, I think your mind and body split apart long ago, in order to protect you from the truth. You've been unknowingly manipulating and harming students ever since, so that you can wage an imaginary war against an imaginary curse — to distract you from what you did to Timothy."

"THAT'S — THAT'S IMPOSSIBLE!" he shouted, but his expression was beginning to show signs of fear and doubt.

The false self was breaking.

"It's not…" I shook my head. "I know you didn't mean to kill him, but you did. His body is right here. The bat you used to kill him is right here."

He began scratching his face frantically. "Timothy — Timothy?"

"Yes…" I said gently. "Timothy. Your son. Your gay son."

He looked down at me desperately, and then in a meek voice that was nothing like the Henrik I had ever heard, he whimpered: "*Help me.*"

"Come down," I said to Henrik, making room for him. "Let me help you."

He scratched his face harder, eyes brimming with tears. Then he nodded and stumbled down into the coffin with me.

"Oh no…" he stammered, running a hand over Timothy's skull. "Oh, Timothy."

"It's okay, Henrik," I said. "You're going to be okay.."

"Oh, Timothy…" he said again, voice growing louder. "What have I done?"

"It's okay…"

"WHAT HAVE I DONE?" he sobbed, grabbing the skeleton in his arms. "OH GOD, WHAT THE HELL HAVE I DONE?"

I closed my eyes as he let out a gut-wrenching scream — the scream of shame that had lived inside of him for so long, desperately trying to claw its way back to consciousness.

As time faded away, he went quiet and cradled the skeleton in his arms, gently brushing his hand where Timothy's red hair once was.

At long last… father and son were reunited.

Eventually, the night sky went red and blue as sirens arrived to end the curse of Lonesome Woods Boarding School.

Jaelyn
Let me out I'm sorry!!!!! Please

WALLS

Golden sunlight danced across campus as we sat in the grass, waiting for the ceremony to begin.

Hundreds of students and teachers were outside during lunch period, chatting excitedly as the crane moved closer to a small sectioned-off zone of the Granite Footpath.

"So what is it gonna be, like... one one-hundredth of the wall?"

"It's symbolic..." I said to Kat. "The rest will take time."

"Symbolic of what?" she asked. "Won't there be *more* walls where crazy Henrik is headed?"

"It's not about where he's going," I said. "It's about where *we're* going. The school is trying to show that his era of paranoia is over — the curse is over."

The crane beeped as construction workers drilled holes into the wall.

"A bit cheesy, don't you think?"

I shrugged.

It *was* a bit of a theatrical gesture from the new headmaster, but I actually appreciated it. I thought it was especially important for the students Henrik had manipulated, to see that the school

115

was changing itself — rather than blaming them.

Henrik had created his own world to escape the real world, and he'd dragged all of us into it — locking us inside with these walls.

It was sad, seeing children get caught up in adult problems. Decades-old trauma had now found a new home in the hearts of twenty-five students. And while destroying a wall would not cure that trauma, it was at least a start.

As for the rest of the healing process…?

Well, that's why they hired me, right?

"Did we miss anything?" Wyatt asked as he helped Oliver down from his crutches.

It was good to see the care-taking roles reversed. I think it gave Wyatt a sense of purpose as he recovered from his addictive habits.

"No," said Kat. "Just some symbolism."

"Oh, I love symbolism!" said Oliver enthusiastically. "What's your favorite symbol? Mine would have to be — well — pretty much anything from the Cyrillic alphabet, I suppose."

"Right," said Kat. "Because that's what I'm talking about."

We talked and bickered, just like any other day at lunch. But it was nice eating outside for a change. Our group hadn't grown yet, to accommodate the loss of Allie and Isabelle, but I had a feeling we'd see some new faces soon.

Eventually, the new headmaster appeared to give some sort of speech about new beginnings and taking down our own walls.

Okay, maybe Kat was right about the cheesy thing.

But when the speech ended and the ceremony finally began, every single one of us watched intently as the small section of the wall came tumbling down.

It was a powerful thing, watching even a tiny part of Henrik's towering structure come crashing to the ground.

Many of the students erupted into cheers, tossing their food and notebooks into the air.

But our group remained mostly silent, looking through the empty space in the wall — out into the world.

I glanced to my side and saw Wyatt reach out to hold Oliver's hand.

And in an even more surprising gesture, Kat leaned her head against my shoulder.

"You did good, Elliot."

I raised my eyebrows. "What? No more daddy?"

"Nah," she said softly. "It got weird."

I laughed. "What changed?"

She paused for a few moments, and then spoke a few simple words that would stay in my heart forever.

"I actually started to see you like a dad… Like the one I never had."

Nicolle
What's going on? Where am I?!

STAY

"Impressive place," said Gabriel, looking around my new suite.

"Thanks," I said, showing him around. "You know, it's amazing how much bigger a space can feel when you don't live with five high school students."

He laughed. "I'm not quite sure how you survived that, actually."

I reached out to hold his hands. "Something tells me you'll make a much better roommate — even if it is just for one night."

He raised his eyebrows. "Elliot, I'm not staying tonight…"

"What?" I said, backing away. "But you're leaving tomorrow."

"Precisely," he said. "I can't stay the night, because I know that you and I will end up…"

His cheeks went pink as his voice trailed off.

I leaned in and kissed him.

"Would that be such a bad thing?" I asked quietly.

"Yes…" he said, kissing me back. "I will not steal your first time, and then wake up to leave you in the morning. You deserve so much more than that."

"You wouldn't be stealing anything," I said, rubbing my hand across the front of his rapidly tightening jeans. "At least let Rafael return the favor..."

He moaned and let out a shaky breath, but then pulled away.

"No, Elliot." He shook his head. "I can't. I won't do it."

My heart sank. Even though I knew he was just trying to protect me, I still felt that horrible pang of rejection.

"Why am I not enough for you?" I blurted out, unable to contain the unbearable storm of emotions raging in my chest.

Gabriel looked at me sadly and held his hand to my heart.

"Elliot, you are more than enough..." he said softly. "You are everything."

"Then why can't you stay?" I said, trying to blink back tears. "Why would you go to New York if I'm everything?"

I felt like I was reverting to some sort of child version of myself.

He brushed a finger along my eyes to dry the tears.

"Elliot you know my leaving is completely unrelated to you. There is nothing left for me in this town."

"The school dropped their lawsuit!" I said desperately. "They lifted your ban from campus. You can bring back the museum!"

"But I don't want that," he said. "I want to do something that brings meaning and purpose to my life, much like the work you've found for yourself."

I bit my lip and nodded.

"I know," I said quietly. "Sorry. It's just... I wish you would stay tonight. I promise I won't make any more moves."

He thought for a moment. "Very well."

"Really?" My eyes lit up.

"Yes," he said with a smile. "I can think of no better way to spend my last night in Lonesome Woods."

I kissed him, and then pulled away. "Wait, we're allowed to kiss right?"

He laughed and kissed me back. "Yes, please."

We made out and rolled around on the bed for what felt like hours, slowly removing more and more clothes. Laying there in our underwear, I had no idea how we were supposed to stop ourselves from taking things further, but I definitely wasn't going to initiate anything.

"So what will you do in New York?" I asked, resting my hand on his chest. "Another museum? The Museum of Modern... Death?"

He laughed and shook his head. "No... No more museums..."

"What about the Lonesome Woods book you're writing?" I said. "You could be a famous New York author!"

"No..." he said again. "I have grown tired of this town's morbid history."

"Then what will you do?" I asked.

"I don't know..." he said. "Something less... gloomy. Maybe a flower shop? Or a bakery!"

That idea seemed to get him adorably excited, like a little kid.

"Bakery it is," I said. "I'd love to come to the city some day and buy a cupcake from you."

"Nothing would make me happier," he said with a smile.

We laid there for a while, dreaming about Gabriel the baker and ignoring the clock at our side — but I knew our time together was running out.

"If I'm to stay the night, allow me a quick shower," said Gabriel. "I've been moving heavy boxes all day, and I can't imagine I'm very pleasant to lay with."

I laughed. "You're fine. But sure, go ahead." I pointed to the bathroom. "The hot water takes a little while. And there's a fresh towel by the sink."

"Thank you." He stood up from bed and leaned down to give me another kiss.

I watched from behind as his perfectly toned back and legs wandered into the bathroom. He left the door slightly ajar, and my heart raced when I saw his beautiful body in the mirror as he began to pull down his briefs.

I doubted that he knew I could see him in the mirror, so it took all of my willpower to avert my eyes out of respect.

While Gabriel showered, I thought about what he might look like in there, dripping in hot water without his underwear on.

That mental image quickly brought my hands to my own boxer shorts.

For the next several minutes, I enjoyed myself to imaginary ideas of Gabriel, desperately hoping that they might become a reality later in the night.

When the shower turned off, I was so worked up that I couldn't help myself.

I had to see. Just once.

So I peeked through the door as he stepped out of the shower, watching in exhilaration as his fully naked body turned to the mirror.

But when I saw his penis, my heart sank — arousal rapidly turning to dread.

There was nothing wrong with it.

It was perfect, just like every other part of him.

But it was crowned by a tuft of bright red hair.

> Mary from New Orleans
> *Wha- Where am I? Wait….Why can't I leave? Hello?! Can anyone hear me?*

My mind raced as Gabriel dried off.

I had nothing against redheads — I loved redheads. But something about this was scaring the hell out of me. We had known each other for a while, and we shared *everything* with each other. Why would he neglect to mention something as innocuous as his natural hair color?

Images of Timothy's red-haired stick figure flashed through my thoughts like cracks of lightning that only grew closer.

No… It wasn't possible. Police had already verified the dental records of the boy from the grave. Timothy was dead.

Gabriel stepped out of the bathroom in his briefs and rejoined me in bed.

"Much better," he said with a smile.

"Good." I said, stilted.

"Now, where were we…?" He wrapped his arms around me. "That's more like it."

I laid there, unmoving.

"Is everything okay, Elliot?" He looked at me.

"Yes," I said. "Sorry. While you were in the shower, I just

started thinking."

"About what?" He kissed my neck.

"Work stuff," I said. It was sort of true.

"You did have quite the week," he said, brushing my hair. "I've been meaning to ask, what ever came of Henrik Small? Does he have a trial set?"

The dread surging through my blood only got worse, screaming at me that something was horribly wrong.

"Not yet," I said, trying to put my therapist hat on. "But whenever it comes, I think I'll be testifying in his favor."

Gabriel stopped kissing my neck. "In his *favor*?"

"Yes." I nodded.

"But... Didn't he hurt all those kids?"

"In a way," I said. "But in a way, he didn't. He was mentally ill. He didn't even know what he was doing."

"Well, he knew enough to kill his son and bury the body." Gabriel's voice was losing its usual calmness. "Is that really mental illness?"

"I think so," I said, taking a deep breath. "In a way, I think Henrik was the victim in all this."

Gabriel's cheeks flushed and his jaw clenched.

"What a stupid thing to say."

I raised my eyebrows, trying to continue playing naive. "What?"

"Sorry," he said quickly and cleared his throat. "It's just, how can he be a victim after what he did to all these people? If anything, he's been exposed as a monster."

"I don't think so," I said, trying to navigate this like a game of chess. "In our final moments together, Henrik told me about his son. It sounded like the boy was a dangerous delinquent."

"LIAR!" Gabriel jumped on me and pinned me to the bed. "YOU'RE LYING!"

I looked up at him, trying to mask my fear.

"Timothy?"

His eyes were wild and fiery, and he pushed me harder into the mattress.

"How did you figure it out?" he demanded.

I blinked and tried to take a deep breath. We were done playing pretend.

"I saw your hair," I said. "In the shower."

He let out an angry sigh.

"Oh, Elliot…" He shook his head. "You've ruined everything."

"I — I don't get it," I said, looking him straight in the eyes. "*Why?*"

Gabriel — or Timothy — thought for a moment, and then finally loosened his hold on me.

"My father… Tried… To KILL me." His voice shook, and his eyes became red. "Twenty-five. FUCKING STRIKES!"

"Twenty-five?" I repeated. "Is that why you recruited twenty-five students to beat Oliver? To recreate your trauma on a similar looking boy?"

Gabriel scoffed. "Trauma? I did it for *justice.*"

"Justice?" I repeated again. "What justice is there in harming innocent students?"

"No one at that miserable school is innocent," he hissed. "You should have seen what they did to me as a child. Drove fucking forks through my hand as a *prank.*"

Well, that explained another one of the incidents.

"But Gabriel… Oliver wasn't even at the school back then."

"THEY'RE ALL THE SAME!" Gabriel slammed his fist on the headboard. "EVERY LAST ONE OF THEM."

"Okay." I nodded, not looking to trigger him further. "So where's the justice?"

He stared at me, as if it should have been obvious.

"To do to my father what he did to me," he said. "To destroy every last semblance of light and happiness in his life. To make him doubt everything about himself. To fill his every waking moment with shame and fear."

I swallowed. "What he did to you was horrible."

"Horrible doesn't begin to describe it!" he roared. "He destroyed me! He left a broken shell of a human. Death would have been better."

I needed to distract him with something less emotionally

charged.

"What about Christopher English?" I asked, working backwards. "Why sentence an old man to death?"

"CHRISTOPHER ENGLISH WAS A DISGUSTING PEDOPHILE!" he screamed. "He gained my trust and raped me — SEVEN TIMES!"

My heart sank. That explained the number seven.

"During the wall incident, the students said 'seven times *father*'. What did Henrik have to do with that?"

"I told him what Christopher was doing to me," said Gabriel, enraged. "He called me a lying whore. So I was Christopher's victim… until I learned how to control him — until I learned how to control everyone."

"How?" I asked.

"I recorded him raping me," he said proudly. "I showed it to him and told him I would share it with his wife and daughter unless he did everything I demanded. From that moment on, Christopher English was my puppet. He helped me disappear. He gave me money to fix my face, after my father destroyed it with a bat. And he told you I was murdered… Directing you to the grave."

"You wanted me to find that body," I thought out loud. "So your father would be sent to prison."

"Yes, Elliot." He wrapped his hand around my throat, but he didn't squeeze. "Christopher English taught me that I can control *anybody* with fear and shame."

"And that's how you got the students to do your bidding…" I said quietly, not wishing to provoke him. "Has it been you all along — the curse?"

"That's right," said Gabriel, tightening his grip. "Every single incident over the years — the murders, the disappearances, the fires, the collapses… Just slutty students afraid of being exposed. And it's gotten a lot easier over the years with social media and phones."

"But my friend traced the phone back to Henrik…" I said, trying to squirm my way out his hold.

"Henrik is a stupid old man who wouldn't understand IP

spoofing even if I explained it to him for the rest of his pathetic life."

I held my tongue, since I was quite sure I wouldn't understand it either.

"But there's one thing that just doesn't make sense…" I said. "They found *your* teeth in that grave."

Gabriel stared down at me, eyes still in a frenzy.

Then he finally took his hand from my throat and stuck it inside his own mouth.

I watched with a mix of horror and disbelief as he removed a pair of dentures — revealing a mouth full of nothing but gums and tongue.

"Do you love me now, *Rafael?*" he said mockingly. "Do you still want me to *stay with you?* Do you still want to be *my everything?*"

"Stop…" I said, heart stinging at my words and feelings being ridiculed like this. "Please, Gabriel. I can help you process all this trauma—"

He leaned down into my face. "Are you trying to *fix* me, Elliot?"

"No!" I protested. "I just… I know you're so tired of being alone, but you're not alone anymore — I'm here. For you."

"God, it's no wonder everyone in your life leaves you," snapped Gabriel — his gaping mouth inches from my own. "You're desperate. Needy. Clingy. Annoying."

"Stop!" I swallowed, no longer able to feign calmness. The words were driving through my heart like knives.

"Of course your father left!" he shouted. "You're nothing but a pathetic nuisance with a burnt cock — irreversibly broken and defective."

"STOP IT, GABRIEL!" I cried.

His eyes lit up with joy, feeding on my fear and shame.

"DO YOU LOVE ME NOW, RAFAEL?" he screeched again, looming closer to me as he opened his mouth wider.

It was like looking into a black hole of disease and suffering.

Then he locked the gaping hole of his mouth onto my mouth and nose, blocking both of my air passages.

"*Mmf*!" I flailed my arms and legs, but I was no match for his strength.

He pinned me down harder and suctioned his gums against the skin on my face, sucking harder and harder — like a reverse form of CPR.

I gasped for air, but none came.

I looked up at him pleadingly, but his eyes were filled with nothing but hatred for me — hatred for everyone in his life who had betrayed him, over and over again.

I tried to take one last breath, but Gabriel would not give it to me.

And soon, everything faded to black.

Mallory from Houma
How did I get here? What am I doing? Where even am I? Who am I?

LIFELESS

"Elliot, wake up!"

The voice echoed in my head, teetering in and out of consciousness.

"ELLIOT!"

Someone was shaking me.

"PLEASE, ELLIOT!"

My blurry vision faded into perspective.

"Kat?" I breathed.

She was standing over me, shaking me hard.

"I'm awake," I said. "I'm — I'm awake."

She stopped shaking me and burst into tears.

"FUCK!" she screamed. "Oh god, what are we going to do?"

"About what?" I asked, still in a daze.

She looked at me, terrified. "About him!"

She pointed at the bed next to me, where — to my horror — I saw Gabriel laying there with a pool of blood around his head.

"What… What happened?" I asked, quickly coming back to reality.

"I came to give you a housewarming gift!" said Kat, sobbing through panicked breaths. "This guy was on top of you. I thought you were having sex, and I was like, *gross*, but *Go Elliot*! But — but he was trying to kill you!"

"Kat, it's okay," I said calmly, sitting up. "What happened next?"

"I hit him!" she cried and pointed to the ground. "With — with your gift. I didn't mean to kill him!"

I looked down and saw a bloody piece of granite on the floor.

"It was supposed to be *symbolic*!" she said. "They were giving out pieces after the ceremony and I thought — I thought you would like it. Oh god, what did I do, Elliot? I'm going to be expelled, aren't I? Or sent to prison?"

"Nothing's going to happen to you," I said firmly. "You didn't do anything wrong, okay? This man was behind everything that happened at the school."

She sniffled and looked up. "Really?"

"Yes," I said. "I'm going to take care of everything. I need you to leave. Go spend the rest of the day with Oliver and Wyatt."

"But — but I killed him!"

"We'll work through that together," I said, thinking fast. "But for now, you need to be with people who can provide an alibi, should it come to that."

Her eyes went wide. "Are you going to go to the police?"

"No," I said truthfully. "We have no way of proving this was self-defense. He had no weapon except his mouth. It's our word against his — and he's dead."

"But people will wonder what happened to him!" she exclaimed. "The police will come looking for him."

"No they won't," I said. "He closed his museum and he was leaving tomorrow for New York City to stay with his non-existent family. Nobody in Manhattan or Lonesome Woods will be looking for him."

She swallowed. "But if he really was behind everything, that means Henrik will go to prison even though he didn't do anything."

I gritted my teeth. "Henrik did plenty to earn his punishment."

"What do you mean?" she asked.

"Kat." I stood up and held her shoulders. "You said you see me as a father. Fathers protect their kids. Let me protect you. Please."

She wiped her eyes and nodded. "O — Okay."

"Go."

She sniffled and ran for the door.

As I knelt over Gabriel's lifeless body, she turned back once from the door.

"Elliot?" she asked meekly. "Where — where are you going to put him?"

I looked up from Gabriel — or Timothy.

"Where he belongs."

Destinee from Chicago
What's going on? I'm scared.

COLD

Our last moment together in the graveyard was unfortunately not a nightmare.

The dirt on the grave was still fresh after the authorities had cremated the skeleton — at Timothy's mother's request — and re-buried an empty grave.

Nobody would notice if it was dug up one last time.

As Gabriel once told me, no one would come looking for a body in a grave that was supposed to be empty.

So I got to work, and unsurprisingly, a half-naked Gabriel stepped from the woods to join me.

"*We're back…*" said Gabriel.

"For the last time," I replied through gritted teeth as I dug harder. "But I'm done talking to a ghost or a memory or a curse — or whatever the hell you are."

"You're angry with me…"

"You tried to kill me!" I hurled a shovel full of dirt at his body. "You made a mockery of my most vulnerable emotions."

"Forgive me…" Gabriel stepped closer to me, abs smeared with dirt. "I was very deeply wounded. I wanted the world to understand my suffering."

"So you made me suffer?" I asked. "What did I ever do to you, except love you?"

Gabriel held his hand to my back. "You did nothing wrong, Elliot… I wanted to accept your love, but I did not know how — because I was broken."

My hands shook as my shovel hit the coffin.

"I could have helped you," I said, eyes burning as I stepped down and opened the coffin.

"So help me…" Gabriel whispered as I pulled his body down with me.

I laid next to Gabriel in the coffin and looked into his eyes.

There was so much hurt and betrayal. Pain that had completely blinded him to the world and to love. A heart filled with so much victimhood that it had accidentally become the perpetrator.

"I can't help you." I brushed his hair. "But I am so sorry. For everything you've experienced."

"Stay with me, Elliot…" he leaned closer, pressing his teeth against my neck. "*Forever.*"

I closed my eyes and thought for a moment.

"No." I shook my head and sat up. "I cannot give any more of myself to you. I have so much to do — a whole life to live."

"You can't go," said Gabriel, eyes watering. "You can't do this to me!"

I held him in my arms. "Everything is going to be okay. No matter what you've done in this life, you will be welcomed back into the great connection."

"You can't leave me like this!" he cried, his voice becoming weak and shaky. "I'm so alone — I'm so… frightened."

Finally, the vampire was gone.

In its place, only a terrified child — created and destroyed by his father.

"I'm sorry, Timothy." I blinked back tears. "I love you so much, but it's time for me to say goodbye."

His body went cold and he collapsed into my arms.

I laid him to rest in the coffin and pulled myself from the grave.

And then, for the last time, I picked up the shovel.

Evan from Chicago
Wait, where am I? How did I get here?

LUNCH

"You guys look happy."

I joined Oliver and Wyatt at lunch the next day, pleased to see them holding hands again.

"My man, Elliot!" Wyatt clapped me on the back and reached out his hand. "What's good?"

It was so nice to see him back to his sober, confident self.

"Boxed lunch as usual?" asked Oliver. "Certainly the safest option when it comes to being assassinated by use of poison."

"Exactly," I said. Then, trying to sound casual, I added: "Anyone seen Kat today?"

"That's my name, don't wear it out." Kat ruffled my hair and took a seat next to me. "Ew, did I just say that? I hate people who say that."

"Kat," I said, looking at her with concern. "How are you doing?"

Wyatt and Oliver went back to flirting and kissing.

"I'm fine..." she said, giving me a funny look. "How are you?"

I lowered my voice. "I took care of everything. You're safe, okay?"

Now she was looking at me like I was insane.

She leaned closer to me and whispered back: "I have no idea what you're talking about."

I raised my eyebrows.

"Kat, you don't have to pretend with me," I said gently. "You don't have to play tough. It's going to take some time, but we'll work through this together."

"Okay." She backed away. "Now, you're freaking me out, Elliot."

What the hell? How was she handling this so easily? She had just killed a man, and she was in complete hysterics last night.

I would have to book some special sessions with her to start diving into the trauma. Perhaps she had blocked it out to protect herself.

Realizing my work was only just beginning, I sighed and opened up my lunchbox.

But looking down, I did not see the ham and cheese sandwich I had packed yesterday.

Inside the lunchbox was only a piece of paper.

A stick figure with red hair — and the message:
RAFAEL

Lei
Hello? Hello? Can anyone hear me? I'm scared...

SPINNING

I stormed into the museum and I felt like I was losing my mind with every passing second.

It wasn't empty.

The walls weren't painted white.

It looked exactly as it had on the day I first visited.

"Elliot! You never called."

My body went cold as Gabriel swooped up next to me.

"*What...*" I whispered. "What are you doing here?"

Gabriel raised his eyebrows. "I beg your pardon? I work here."

I felt like I was looking at a ghost.

What was happening? Why was he acting like we barely knew each other?

"You're supposed to be dead..." I said in disbelief.

Gabriel gave me a funny look.

"I am going to assume you are not interested in dinner, then?"

What the hell?

"Dinner? You — you tried to kill me!"

Gabriel started to back away. "I'm sorry?"

"And you…" I spun around, pointing at the walls. "You repainted this whole museum! You put everything back where it was."

Gabriel stared at me, confused. "Is everything okay, Elliot?"

"No, it's not okay!" I said, raising my voice. "What the fuck is going on? Why are you pretending like last night never happened? Why are you pretending like *we* never happened?"

Gabriel's expression went from one of confusion — to one of apprehension.

"Elliot, I think I'm going to ask you to leave," he said nervously. "You're making me uncomfortable."

"No!" I said, lunging forward and grabbing him by the throat. "You do not get to walk free after what you did to those kids! I will bury you again if I have to."

Gabriel's eyes went wide as he tried to fight me off.

I squeezed harder until he began to choke.

I was done with his mind games and lies. This time, I would finish the job.

I glared straight into his eyes, watching as they became red and teary — bulging and begging me to stop.

"*Elliot… Please…*"

As soon as the words escaped his mouth, my entire body suddenly became overwhelmed by a familiar heavy, dizzy sensation.

My hands went weak and Gabriel backed away, gasping for air.

I tried to grab him again, but the whole room started to spin…

And then I collapsed.

Nick from Boulder
Please I can't leave

CONCLUSIONS

"Have I gone insane?"

"No, Elliot... But you may have to choose between two realities."

My childhood therapist, Dr. Cole, peered at me through a pair of glasses and crossed her legs after listening to me talk for an hour straight.

Following my breakdown at the museum, Gabriel called the police, and she was the only person I could think to bail me out. I wasn't in touch with my parents, and Zach would have given me that obnoxious holier-than-thou look.

"What do you mean?" I asked, desperate for answers.

"Well in one reality, you have this mastermind psychopath who lusted after you unconditionally, nearly smothered you to death with his gums, placed strange drawings in your lunchbox, pretended to close and reopen his museum to trick you, removed his teeth and faked his own death like a television crime drama—"

"I get it," I said, embarrassed. "It sounds crazy. But what other explanation is there?"

She looked up from her notebook. "The simple one, Elliot."

"What?" I asked. "How could any of this be simple?"

"I'm assuming you're familiar with avoidant personality disorder?"

"Gabriel didn't have that," I said quickly. "He was never afraid of rejection. He pursued me — fearlessly."

"I'm not talking about Gabriel," she said. "I'm talking about you."

I frowned. "AVPD? I don't — I don't have that."

She sighed. "Elliot. I'm going to be candid with you, now that we're both adults with psych degrees. I made this diagnosis long ago — on the day we first met."

"*What?*" I whispered. "Why?"

"Your father's abandonment left you with a crippling fear of rejection," she said. "A constant, deep feeling of inadequacy that we never got a chance to explore. You just decided to jump right into saving people instead — a distraction from the pain. As a healer, you feel safe from rejection because you don't have to be vulnerable, and others *need* you."

I shook my head in disbelief, but I wanted to hear more.

"For the sake of argument, let's say you're right," I said. "What does any of that have to do with Gabriel?"

She held my eye contact. "Elliot, did anyone ever *see* you with Gabriel?"

"Yes, of course—" I said. But then I thought for a moment. "Well... No. I mean, I guess there was one waitress for a few seconds. What are you getting at?"

She paused for a moment. "Many people with untreated AVPD tend to develop elaborate fantasies, to fill the void of a broken inner world. These fantasies often include relationships... Imaginary relationships that allow them to fall in love without the risk of becoming vulnerable — without the risk of being rejected again and re-triggering the painful feelings of inadequacy."

"Fantasies?" I said in disbelief. "Are you suggesting I invented Gabriel in my mind? Because I can take you to meet him right now."

"I believe that he exists," said Dr. Cole calmly. "But I'm not sure you ever saw him again after your first visit to the museum."

My heart sank. "What? How can you say that?"

"That day, you met an exceptionally attractive man who asked you out on a date," she said. "Rather than risk exposing yourself to more rejection, after your previous boyfriend — Will — called you *desperate*, is it possible that you created a fantasy relationship with Gabriel?"

"No!" I said, shaking my head. "No, it's not possible. I mean, vampire Gabriel was obviously in my imagination, but the rest was real."

"Are you certain, Elliot?" she asked. "Because Gabriel seemed to have quite a bit of *you* in him. Interest in psychology and spirituality... Wounds from his own father... Disfigured from childhood scars... A desire to heal you..."

"That was..." My voice trailed off, feeling less and less certain of myself by the moment. "What about the bad stuff? Why would I invent a relationship with a secret vampire who tried to kill me?"

"Might that be the manifestation of your emotional wounds, sucking away your life force?" she suggested. "Toward the end, you described Gabriel almost exactly as you once described the demon from your childhood nightmares... Do you remember that, Elliot? *A black hole of disease and suffering.*"

My body filled with dread as I realized she was right.

"So... if that wasn't Gabriel, what was it?"

"The shadow self," said Dr. Cole simply. "The part of you that is repressed and unfelt. The deeply painful parts of your identity that you have yet to process. So you projected them onto Gabriel, to feel them for you. Left untended, these dark emotions will always inevitably rise to the surface and poison your fantasies until their message is heard."

"So... Henrik really *was* behind everything?"

"That would be the simple explanation, yes."

"But..." I bit my lip. "What if you're wrong? What if Gabriel did all of these awful things to the school, and he's still out there? What if everything was real up until the part where Kat killed him? What if he just left me there unconscious, and put the note in my lunchbox?"

"That's where your choice comes into play," said Dr. Cole. "You are the one who decides which reality to believe."

"I can't just choose — I need an answer!"

Dr. Cole gave me an apologetic smile.

"The only way to get a definitive answer would be to pull down Gabriel's pants and verify the color of his pubic hair. As your therapist — and the person who just posted your bail — I would advise against that."

"So what *would* you advise?"

"I would advise you to begin the healing process that you never began," she said gently. "Real or fantasy, Gabriel gave you some sound wisdom — you formed false conclusions about yourself based on your father's departure. So begin to explore those conclusions. Feel the intolerable emotions and shame that the event imparted on your psyche. And then let it all go... Because I promise you, Elliot, it *is* false."

I leaned back in the chair, my mind completely scrambled as I tried to comprehend what Dr. Cole was telling me. On one hand, it seemed far-fetched and impossible. But on the other hand, it made a lot more sense than *my* explanation, which was much more far-fetched and impossible.

I was quite familiar with AVPD, and everything she was describing could actually apply to me.

I just... I couldn't believe I never noticed it in myself. I couldn't believe I had such an active imagination. I couldn't believe my mind and heart were working so hard to distract me — or perhaps, to protect me.

Dr. Cole leaned forward and placed her hand on mine.

"Are you feeling okay?"

"Yes," I said quietly. "I think so."

"What are you thinking?"

"I don't know..." I said truthfully. "It makes sense. It really does. I guess it all just seems so... dramatic."

"Elliot..." she said with a smile. "You've always had a flare for the dramatic."

Oscar from Around

Do you believe that hell was made to appear familiar at first glance? What might look like a school... a prison, an island retreat, a psych office... might only be a facade to give its captives false hope? After all, when in hell, one finds oneself in communion with an odd swarm of demons...

EPILOGUE

I entered my office and dropped my bags on the ground. I flipped on the small desk lamp and opened the shades to reveal another rainy day.

I smiled. The weather didn't bother me anymore. In fact, I think I liked the rain.

Relaxing back into my chair, I looked around the room and let out a deep breath.

It was good to be back.

I had taken a few weeks of personal leave to begin the healing process. I still had a lot of work to do, but I felt like I was making good progress.

I was just starting to experiment with feeling those uncomfortable emotions, and catching them with mindfulness so they wouldn't consume me.

It was hard work, but it was work worth doing.

And interestingly, as I changed myself, I found my entire outlook on life changing.

For example, I realized I didn't even want to be with someone like Gabriel anymore — the suave, mysterious, seductive healer. I didn't want to be in a relationship that was all about mending each other's wounds.

I wanted someone real. Someone kind, someone flawed… and maybe a little awkward.

But for now, I was content with being single. I was just getting started, and I didn't want to re-enter the dating pool until I was happy with myself.

As for the school?

I could handle the school now. Henrik was gone. The incidents had stopped.

It was just a normal job now. A "glorified guidance counselor", as Henrik had once called me. The students and teachers held a lot of respect for me these days, and the campus was more beautiful than ever without the wall.

I know it sounds crazy, but I could actually see myself sending my future kids to this school someday.

I was finally starting to feel *good* about myself for the first time in a long time. Which meant I felt ready to help students with their issues because I genuinely cared, not because I was trying to distract myself or save them.

As I began unpacking my things, the door creaked open.

"Hey, I need to talk with you." A scrawny boy in a hoodie approached my desk, keeping his head bowed down. "You're the therapist, right? Dr. Harper?"

I closed my desk drawer and gave him an encouraging smile. "You can call me Elliot."

"Sure, okay." His voice was fast and agitated. "So there's a girl I really like. But I think she's leading me on. She's really nice to me when we're alone. But then around her friends she's a huge bitch. She acts like she's better than me. She acts like she's some sort of queen, and I'm just here to serve her. I think someone needs to put her in her place."

"Wow, okay! I'm glad you came to me." I took out my notebook, finally ready to begin helping these kids. "Before we dive into things, I don't believe we've had the pleasure of meeting. What's your name?"

He slowly looked up from his hoodie, and I saw two dark eyes — filled with endless rage.

"Alex."

GET THE NEXT BOOK

I'm a Therapist, and My Patient is Going to be The Next School Shooter

on Amazon.com

PREVIEW THE FORTHCOMING CROSSOVER BOOK

Return to Lonesome Woods

Some say Lonesome Woods Boarding School traumatizes and wounds its students.

Others believe that Lonesome Woods Boarding School *attracts* the traumatized and the wounded.

Like a siren luring in sailors at sea, the school seems to entice fractured souls onto its dreary campus, over and over again.

A dark place for healing and self-exploration, its inhabitants struggle to leave the school until they face the shadow within.

Perhaps that's why a rebellious young student went on to become the school's headmistress.

Perhaps that's why a Civil War enthusiast decided to become the school's next history teacher.

Perhaps that's why a recovering addict accepted a role as the school's athletics director.

Perhaps that's why a museum curator never left town.

And perhaps, many years later, that is why I chose to send my son to Lonesome Woods Boarding School.

* * *

James was reported missing from campus thirty-six hours ago.

I know it's my fault.

But there's no sense in wallowing in the past — that's what Noah says anyway.

We have to find him now. That's all we can do.

Yes — we.

I'm going to need all the help I can get.

Noah, Kierra, and Zach are in the car with me as we drive to Lonesome Woods.

It's pouring rain and thundering. Everyone is silent.

I look at Noah, and I can see he's as frightened as I am.

There is a flash of lightning, and suddenly I see a familiar vampire in Noah's place.

I blink, and he is Noah again.

I fear that I have yet to face my shadow.

ARE YOU READY TO RETURN?

visit DrHarperTherapy.com

LONESOMEWOODS.ORG

GUESTBOOK ENTRIES
...be sure to read the last entry...

Elliot from Lonesome Woods
Miss you Gabriel... See you tonight. ♡

Henrik from Lonesome Woods
Fuck you and your disgusting museum.
Stop exploiting children who are
VICTIMS OF A CURSE!!

Belle from Lonesome Woods
Thanks for all the help Gabriel! I always
learn so much from you. Wishing you
well with your book. Hello world :)

Sasha
excuse me what is this

Olivia from Glasgow
I am scared. Who are you Gabriel?
What happened to Noah?

Jade from Chesterfield
Wheres Noah? What have you done to
him Gabriel?!

heather from camden
shout out to my boyfriend!

Everett
FIRST.

Diana
Who are you and what are you going to
do? Leave us alone.

Robert from Lonesome Woods
Can't wait for the new year to start...

see you soon Gabriel!

Diana
Who are you and what are you going to
do? Where's Noah?! WHERE IS HE YOU
CREEP

Paulina from Exeter
Hello, I'm lost, where are we ?

Andrew from Bath
Go home, Dr. Harper. You're drunk
again. Noah will help you back to sleep

Cameron from Gold Coast
Where am I?

Mel from Sedona
Just remember buddy. If you kill Noah,
we riot.

KP
Soooo.... This is unsettling.

Julia from Kansas City
Please put me in the book!!!! I love your
series and am freaking out. Hi to Bri for
introducing me to your books!!

Kai
Where the hell are we?

Jess
stop playing games with our hearts! you
are retired in the mountains. i forbid
you from visiting this school

Noah
WTF Who is Gabriel???

Sam from Cape May
HYPE

Angela
Please tell me you don't live in this museum. I want to read the whole book and not have it end with your early death.

Katarina
Dearest Gabriel, Looking forward to seeing you again. Did you think I had forgotten about you? Or your secrets?

Kas
Dr. Harper I came here because I need help, could you finally listen to me??

Sean
Check it out mama Sean is in a book!

Ashley from Lonesome Woods
Excited to read this - I've been looking forward to learning more :)

Chantelle from Scottish Borders
Noah you okay dude?

Craig
Why you sending hearts to another boy? Unacceptable doc!!

Megan from Scottish Borders
Dr Harper you better not break Noah's heart :(

Brienna from Kansas City
JULIA!!!!!! LETS GO.

Trev from Orlando
ummmmmmm what are you getting us into here

Kaylan
Where are we? I don't even remember the ride here. Gabriel, what have you done? Why are we here? What is this book about? If it's about.....you know,

so help me God, I'll kill you.

Krina from Las vegas
What is going on? This should have never happened!

God from Heaven
Elliot this is God and I am commanding you to stop it with this Gabriel chap

Terra from The North
Very intriguing. Looking forward to reading about the school Gabriel.

rebecca
doc this is cruel and unusual

Montse
Let families grieve in peace you fucking moron

Nikki
This place gives me the creeps... and not the good kind...

Leo from Brisbane
Doc if you could not do this when I'm about to fall asleep that would be cool

Luca from São Paulo
Oh well, here we go again

Hiu
Elliot... I love and hate you so very much. Why do you do this to us.

Ava from Nice
This is giving me the spooks

James
How could you do this to me! You have a husband and son you ass

LaRenn from Seattle
Noah better be ok or I'll be very upset!

Trey from Dallas
My teacher hates this series so much, so shout out to Mrs. Brennan

Evan from Chicago
Wait, where am I? How did I get here?

Grace from London
I'm so excited!!! My friends and I read all of your books in our reading club and we're all losing our minds in group chat

Craig from Hauppauge
Excited for this story to be shared and for new souls to visit.

Vio from NYC
You must have brainwashed Dr. Harper. He would never cheat on Noah. We will find you and free him.

Sam
Do you enjoy toying with us or...

Jasmine from Charlotte
this is so fun and weird and confusing

Mallory
I don't plan on visiting this museum...

KVD from Somewhere
Putting my initials to check in later :)

Sandy from Burford
NOPE. Nope nope nope. Not visiting your museum. Stay away from our therapist.

Mia
If this really shows up in a book I just want to say I love my pup

Dee
I see your getting yourself into trouble again... Sigh.

Olivia
I am torn between wanting more of your books and wanting you to leave Elliot and Noah alone.

Sally from North Yorkshire
I'm a spiritual medium and I'm outa here! There's something in the toilets that keeps shoving toilet roll down your pants when you flush!

Damian from Krakow
I have read all of your books and will read this one too but I am getting really nervous vibes right now

Catherine from West Coast
Leaving a note for the book... Hope I don't regret this. :-I

Corey from Edinburgh
This is totally normal. No need for concern.

Alexis from Pittsburgh
Be careful everyone, especially Elliott, this seems sketchy.

Pooja
Gabriel with respect you are not giving me the best impression right now

Keysha from Atlanta
Damn what are you doing!

Laura from London
This sure looks like a long and fun ride.

Skyler from Enfield
What happened??!!!

Dr.
This looks like a wonderful school! Are they hiring a principal?

ankkit
can anybody please tell me what is going on

Ceren from Istanbul
I've never liked the idea of boarding schools and I guess I was right.

Danica from Lancaster
Sounds super suspicious and super intriguing. I wonder what secrets the school holds?

evelyn
why gabriel?!

Lei
Hello? Hello? Can anyone hear me? I'm

scared...

Jordin
Uh oh. This seems not good

Isaac
I met my forever love, Maddie, in this school!

Maddie
Thank you for your help Gabriel, wishing you well on your future endeavors.

Dawn from Cannon Beach
Sure haunted boarding schools are cool and all. But you know what else is cool? Living out your remaining days in peace with a family who loves you very much. Just a thought?

Brittany from Kenmare
YESSSSSS BRING IT ON!!!!!

Rachel
Love you Max ♡♡♡♡

Sammie
Help

Richard
Guys I think I figured it out. Doc leaked a teaser here:
https://www.youtube.com/watch?v=dQw4w9WgXcQ

Sabine from Highsand
I wish all the best to you

Doug
It seems the museum is missing history - everything that happened before the school was built. The plague of 1992 that wiped out half the wildlife. The destruction of the shrine. The contaminated deer "incident." Is all of this being covered up / forgotten?

Taishiro
Doctor this does not seem like a man you should be spending time with

Stephanie from Yellow Springs
I'm looking forward to visiting your museum, Gabriel. I am one of the lost souls. Perhaps you can help welcome me back ;)

Ella from Jonesboro
Hi everyone! I'm in a book!

Elliot
Elliot, this is your conscience speaking. Turn back now. Red flags all about. Have a lovely day!

Brian
Ummm where am I

Shalyse
HOW COULD YOU KILL MY SON!

Jayy
What is the Museum and who are the souls wandering... what's going on ?

Melanie from Brisbane
Oh Elliot dear. This looks delightful and gross, as always.

Kodie
Help me

Larissa from The Netherlands
Very exciting there is a new book on it's way! Can't wait to get myself lost in the thrilling chapters!

Jasmine from London
I know, I know who did it.

Lauren from Redcar
Hi

Mrs.McLachlan
Gabriel you need to get out now before it's too late! Beware of the room with walls of blood red.

Amber from Lonesome Woods
Learn from the past. History repeats itself. :)

Caroline from New Orleans

OMG WHAT THE HELL IS THIS

vicky
Bring it on?

Caroline
Gabriel? Is that really you? We used to laugh so well together…

Desiree
I don't like this at all…..

Jordan from Portland
Well this looks interesting; who doesn't love a good haunting?

Jonathan
This is extremely intriguing and cannot wait to read this book

Katie from Stockport
Help, it's dark and I can't get out!

Taylor from Lonesome Woods
I escaped this school. No one in my new life knows this. But I'll let you all in on a little secret. Those of Lonesome Woods KNOW what is going on at that boarding school. I'll curse my parents forever for putting me through what they did.

A
Hello Gabriel. I'm presuming you've done something with Noah. Elliott will find you. From, A friend of Noah

Natalie from Winston Salem
These woods are very lonesome.. Thank you for giving my soul a voice!

Marie from London
Wow I can't believe it, finally…I've been waiting so long for this!

Michelle from Glasgow, Scotland
Excited to see where this one goes…

Katie from Buffalo
Ooooo!!!!! Please don't die. So excited!!!!!!

Maggie from San Francisco
I AM PANICKING. HURRY, SOMEONE CALL A THERAPIST. OH WAIT.

Kate from Torbay UK
Fascinating. Unsettling. Curious. Love it!!

Tori from Auburn GA
Hiiiiii

Kevin from Trebbin
I can still remember seeing this place in the news. It was a report about the classroom fire that killed the 5 kids. I came to get my kid and seeing the parents of those children cry… I thought about that for a long time man.

Tori from Auburn GA
Noah better be okay!

Brent from London
Well this is a lovely thing to receive as the sun goes down. Thanks bunches Elliot.

Mars
…

Heather from Loogootee
Love the museum! Happy and willing to help souls get to rest!

Mallory
just wanted to be a part of this :)

Ava from Lonesome Woods
stay far away from this place, they want you to visit but what ever you do DO NOT COME NEAR if you ever wish to leave again

cyrus
fuck this and this school

Chloe from Earth
Who are you and what have you done to Noah?!? (Can't wait for the book!)

Nicolle
What's going on? Where am I?!

Meghan from Lonesome Woods
What a very interesting boarding school this is looking to be, I'm glad Gabriel decided to give a voice to lost souls, although I'm not sure they needed one...

Jada
Can I attend? Nice to meet you, Gabriel.

Simon from London
BEWARE....

Emily from Niagara Falls
Gabriel, where is Noah? What is your story Gabriel? I'm excited to get to know you.

Roxxi
Where's Noah? Who's Gabriel? Why am I bleeding?

Squeak
I haven't seen another living person since arrival.. what is this place? They said it was haunted, but I never believed in ghosts.. I was so wrong, please forgive me.

Jordyn from Sedalia
Gabriel...what have you done with noah>:(

Rachel from London
ENTER AT OWN RISK..

Aleynia
Please let me out! This smoke is so thick. I'm choking and everything is burning. I want to go home. I miss my parents. I don't want to be stuck here forever. I'm so scared.

Harry from Exeter
Consider this, Timothy Small never left the school, surely a museum curator is the perfect job to avenge your suffering

Ronnie
Stay Away From the Children

Andraea from Butte MT
I'm in college to become a therapist! Someday I hope to have all the dangerous mind boggling adventures that Dr. Harper has! Well... not really.

Erin from Lonesome woods
I hope to be the next story in this dark history's collection.

Jamie from Arlington
I'm Scared! What is this!? Hello all! :p

Brianna from Phoenix
Bri wuz here LOLZ missing doc and noah

Ryan from New York City
I heard there was a curse and I came RIGHT AWAY

Jeep
Electricity went out within ten minutes of arriving. Some members of our group began experiencing thoughts that could not be explained no matter how you tried. One of the men began singing in an odd high-pitched voice sitting alone near the far corner. His voice was normally deep and manly but sounded like a woman singing. I am not sure what happened. I will not be returning.

Jenn from The Asylum
Every time I reach the exit, I'm back at the entrance with a horrible new tale to follow. Who would ever wish to leave this wonderfully terrifying place?

Eleanor from Manchester
Love these books! Can't wait for the new one

Bee
Seriously, why am I still here this place gets on my nerves and scaring people isn't even fun anymore. Gabriel can you do something I don't even care about acknowledgment just get me the hell out of here. Seriously hell would be better.

Alanis from North West England
My guess is that teenagers are weird and there is no understanding them. (Probably a cult)

Bruno from Łódź
To anyone who's reading this: Have a nice day <333

Dawn
See you soon!!

Danni from Niskayuna
So excited to meet you Gabriel!I know Dr Harper will be too. Can't wait to see what happens next.

Sarah from Florence
I cannot wait to interact with the wandering souls, Gabriel. Thank you for this hauntingly splendid opportunity. As always, stay well old friend.

Alex from Sheffield
What's going on?

Kaylee from Cleveland
I can't wait to see what horrors await us!

Megan from Spring city
I am intrigued, very intrigued

Ashley from Who knows
I doubt anyone will be able to see this, but if you'd do... don't trust what you hear. NOTHING is safe

Ash
hi bye

Robyn
Creepy ghosts and documentation of it? Very exciting!!

S+R♡ from South East
Thought it would be a good date night location as we love scary stuff but upon arrival we got more than what we bargained for... Words can't even describe... the nightmares still haven't stopped I'm beginning to think they

never will...

James from Dudley
If anyone is reading this I just want to say I love you Debbie and maisie

Jennifer from Stockport
Don't go there ..... some things should be left alone !!!

Pac from Liverpool
Gabriel, Do you recognise the bodies in the water? Have you ever seen the bodies in the water before? Gabriel... you do not recognise the bodies in the water.

Leanne from Newcastle upon Tyne
Dr Harper. We need your help... something strange is happening in my town...

Danielle
Please be safe, wherever you go next. I don't want anything bad to happen to you or your loved ones if you all explore this creepy place. Stay safe, please.

Lexi from Lexington
We will find out the truth...

Maria from Shelby Township
Hauntings are 100% real, whether or not we witness them. Some are just...unrested.

Rebekkah from Cullowhee
Where did everyone go? I came to meet Gabriel and now he's gone...

Amiya
What happened to me ? I entered the building and I felt like a fell through a portal...

Alex from London
Very excited to learn more

Stacey from Holiday, Florida
It's so sad how much bad much this school has had. Prayers to the families left behind.

Orion
Hey so like I just woke up... any explanation??

Ariel from Lonesome Woods
For anyone unfortunate enough to be a current student at LW, I have only one word of advice: check under your bed every night before you go to sleep. Sincerely, one of the surviving alumni

Carrie
My uncle Ed suggested this school to me, he was right it was a great start to my career as a serial killer......

Floyd from West Jefferson
Umm, yeah that's right....

Donna from Morgantown, WV
Is this museum offering haunted tours? I'd be interested in that. Also...what happened to Noah???

Angela from Talladega
Thanks for letting us visiting, but something felt off and spooky. As if someone was breathing in my ear. I heard silent screams in the walls "help us!" The sound of children playing in the halls but there was no children

Danielle from Loma Linda CA
Love all Dr. Harper's books! Can't wait to read the new book & see what happens next :)

Tom from New York
to be honest i have no idea whats going on right now

Liv from Kent
Oh boy this is getting good! I have loved all your books :) I'm excited to read this, although I want to know: where's Noah and where is Lonesome Woods Boarding School??

Eden from Melrose
Why would you create a museum for the lost souls? This is all very suspicious, Gabriel.

Azur
Hmm...interesting. I'm a fan of haunted places. I'll keep my eye on this.

Hannah from Wiltshire
Where am I? and how did I get here??

Tonya from Fort Leavenworth
Hi Gabriel. To truly know our story, you must join us on the other side. Come to us.

Gage from Lawrence
I know your secret Gabriel, and I will never forget.

Bridgette from Plano
Dear Gabriel, what happened to Noah I know you have more to tell and we all want to know. I hope you haven't done anything terrible.

Amy from Basildon
Can't wait to meet you Gabriel ♥

Sarah from Morristown
You're doing great work. Stories need to be told and I'm happy to be a part of those lucky enough to absorb them.

Dianna from Austin, TX
Such a terrible thing. They were so young. WHY did this happen...

Courtney from Nebraska
So many chills and so many questions. Gabriel, I hope you can answer them.

Gemma from Fleetwood UK
So much eeriness

klaire from pensacola
gabriel i think you should stop now

Rimneet
Ah hello, i'm not sure what I am doing here but here I am, please Gabriel. Let me go.

Simone

I can't believe something so heinous and strange could happen right under people's noses like this... Something needs to be done, and fast.

Caitlin
Doc this is unconventional even for you

Caitlin
Leave the ghosts of the victims of this place alone

Katrina
Hey Dr, ready for our appointment?

Deidre from Virginia Beach
Tell Noah we'll be seeing him soon...

Alicia from Antioch
I can't wait to visit the museum...and stay awhile?

Beth from Portsmouth
I hope Noah is still here.. he saved your ass so many times

Samara from Somerset
Who's this Gabriel? Who's Elliot? I just want to go home!

Megan
help

Lauren from Canterbury
Thank you for documenting these goings-on, Gabriel - perhaps we can finally find out exactly what causes these horrors!

Stephanie
Im so excited for this!!! eeekkk

Diamond
How creepy

Mackenzie from Cecil Hotel
Why oh why did I make my mother let me go on the school field trip to Skid Row.. damn the homeless..

Ella from Tacoma
Gabriel, who is Noah? And why am I

suddenly feeling cold all of a sudden.... There's blood dripping on my screen of this site & I don't know if it's real or not... please send help.

Airi from Pennsylvania
Looking forward to being very haunted....and entertained!

Moriah
Welcome back Dr. Harper. We knew you couldn't stay away for long.

Jayden from Omaha
Everywhere you go, mischief and mystery seems to follow

Terry
Oh god. Why?

Stacy
Why are you here? We don't want you here. We don't want anyone here. You will see. Soon. You will see...

Megan from Northern California
While visiting this page I felt a surge if spirit energy.

DeShan from Smithville
During a student council meeting, I noticed their odd behavior. The eyes are what I noticed first. Slits instead of pupils! Cold. So cold were their bodies. I offered snacks, but all they could do stare. Slowly, they tried approaching; closer and closer. I backed away and ran faster than I thought possible. I don't think these students were students at all.

Çınar from Manisa
Oh Gabriel, this won't be our last encounter my friend, watch your back.

Femke
I do love visiting museums... Maybe it won't hurt to visit this place. Hopefully it won't hurt.

Aiden from Lonesome Woods
To anyone reading this DO NOT VISIT

THE MUSEUM OR THE SCHOOL. I
repeat, DO NOT VISIT THIS
GODFORSAKEN PLACE.

Sami
WHY?!?!?!?!? I NEED TO KNOW!!!!!

Kymeshia from Weston Super Mare
What is going on here? Gabriel?
GABRIEL?!?!

Chloe from Norwich
What the hell is going on here...see you
in hell

Nick from Boulder
Please I can't leave

Raven
I dont like this one bit. Like im legit
really creeped out right now.

Georgia from Hereford
I just know your next book will be
amazing just like all your other books.
I've been a long time fan, looking
forward to it!

Lauren from Manchester
What happened to Noah??? How is this
related to a museum? Please give us
answers

Carly-Simone from Uk
Sooo excited got the next adventure to
begin!!

Madi from Tacoma
Oh Gabriel I love spooky history stuff
like this it keeps me on edge. Looking
forward to know more information
about the school. Also love the dripping
blood nice little surprise.

Anna from Detroit
Eager to see you, it's been awhile!
Forever yours Anna

Emily
Omg so excited for the new book! Love
the series so much!!

Mary from New Orleans
Wha- Where am I? Wait....Why can't I
leave? Hello?! Can anyone hear me?

Michelle from Philadelphia
The students need to be heard. Even
those no longer with us

null from pizza hut
hey who ordered this pizza

Rebecca from Pleasant Valley
Arson or could it be spontaneous
combustion?

Xavier from Lonesome Woods
I survived the collapse. I can assure you
it was no accident. The night it
happened, I awoke to a voice
whispering in my ear "and it all comes
tumbling down". Still paralyzed to this
day.

Ashley from The South
Elliot, Noah needs you. Don't do this...
please...

Kylee from SLC
I cannot wait for your new book, my
fiance and I are looking forward to
reading it together!

Lorena from Edinburg
I love all Dr. Harper book series!! I been
waiting for this masterpiece to be
released for months!!! Couldn't be more
excited!

Anouther
Please don't exploit a tragedy for cash.
But what would I expect from a
crapitalist. Aside from that, cool
museum, very fun when you're on acid.
?

Daria
Gab..riel? Who are you? And what am I
doing here? What is this place? And
why is it so cold...?

heather from new jersey
DOC!!! PLEASE PUT ME IN THIS BOOK

IM OBSESSED

Totianna
Elliot where's Noah? WHAT HAPPENED TO THE SWEETHEART NOAH!?

Jasmine from Georgia
I want to be part of history, never forgotten.

Mallory from Houma
How did I get here? What am I doing? Where even am I? Who am I?

Eve
Ashes, ashes. We all fall down

Beth from Chester
Im soe excited for this. Mossy - you better be up to date!

Kimberly from Atlanta
What's happening here????

Brenna from Lonesome Woods
What did you do with him?!

Abraham
Something fishy going on here

Jasmine from Visalia
I was going to win 2008 prom queen.. but now I keep reliving a horrible death. What happened to me? And have you seen my prom date Jorge?

BPR
Signing for the book

Rayanna
Noah???? Elliot????

Freida from London
This seems like a dangerous place Elliot. You sure you want to be here?

Drew
Jessica!

Erin from Seattle
Cant wait!!

Peter from LonesomeWoods
Lost many friends at my time here. Not sure a museum is in very good taste. I will never step foot in this school again

adrian
doc im screaming ive missed you so much

Deirdre from Cedar Key
This is very intriguing. I can't wait to meet you, Gabriel.

Sarah
Where is Noah??

Kyle
Put my in the book please

pee
cock

Jenifer
I can't wait to hear from you Gabriel, and hear what you and the other students have been up to.

Jaylyn
HELLO?! WHERE AM I?! NOAH?! ARE YOU PRANKING ME?! WHERE IS EVERYONE?!

Lauren from Kingston
Thanks for everything, Gabriel! My time at the museum was a scream! Might wanna do something about the some of the permanent residents, though, they won't stop crying. Just a thought. Good luck with your book!

Mai
I keep seeing Timothy in my dreams ever since coming here. How do I make it stop. The moment I close my eyes his face haunts me.

Loocim from Miami
um i dont know what this is but i cant wait.

Charlotte
What happened to Noah? what have

you done to him!

Betty
I can't believe one school was the place of so much tragedy in such a short time. There has to be some sort of conspiracy about this. What if I'm next. Oh god don't let me be next. I should never have come here.

Sam from Ogden, UT
Interesting way to kill an hour or two...I don't know there's some weird vibes...like you can feel the pain and fear? I... I wish I hadn't come.

Scout from Carlisle
Looks nice here, although it has that "you can check out anytime you like, but you can never leave" vibe.

M from Lonesome Woods
Don't go. Those lucky enough to escape have spoken. Stay away from LW. Once you enter, you'll never get back out. Stay as far away as you can, please. I don't want it to happen again.

Kayte from Holyoke
This was amazing! Please tell me there's an after hours haunting tour??

Becky from Southampton, UK
This is so intense, can't wait!

Elle from Wishaw
Wow ! Aren't you good at treating the crazies, well it takes one to know one ...

Hannah
I LOVED the prom dress exhibit! My favorite part was climbing through the collapsed dorm! Super excited with my souvenir sipper! I'll never leave.... Help me.... I *can't* leave... Help?

Carrie from Norwich
Anxious, excited, I need to know more!

Makayla from New York
Glad to see you back, Doc. Always a pleasure to hear about your work. Can't wait to read the newest files. Gabriel, watch your back. Take good care of Elliot. Lonesome Woods holds many secrets and dangers. Don't trust anything. I hope you're out there with Elliot, Noah. You bring the best out of him. Stay close to him.

Kay
Who are you, Gabriel? Where is Noah? What are you going to do to us? Stay safe and watch your back... You never know what can happen...

Sophie from London
I'm here to find out what happened to my sister, WhT are you hiding Gabriel, what did you do to them...

Chloe from London
STILL not the worst school I've been to! Do they have any vacancies for a History teacher?

Phoebe from Manchester
Gabriel, what have you done...

Zoe from Stroud uk
Dr Harper we are relying on your professional and not so professional skills to get to the bottom of what is happening. If anyone can sort this out you can. Take care and watch your back

Amy from Manchester
Gabriel is sus

dani from Wichita Falls
i have no idea what the fuck is happening but i wish i was part of the suicide pact.

Chelsea from Fort Wayne
What is this exactly? Looking forward to reading this

Allen from Huntington
I love Dr. Harper and I'm so excited about a new book. A haunted school/museum.. what could go wrong. Can't wait!

Kenna
Everyone stay away! I was here, and I will never forget...

Christine from Fountain
I was apart of the suicide pack but lived. And now I speak for all in the suicide pack.

Jax from Mississippi
I'm in a book teehee

Chloe from London
STILL not the worst school I've visited! Any vacancies for a History teacher?

Victoria
Beware Gabriel, your life is in danger!

Zoey
I like your funny words magic man

Frog
11/28/2020 <3

Kelsey from Belton
H-How did I get here? Somebody, please help! It's dark in here and I can't move for the ropes binding me!

Brianna from Bella Vista
Very excited to see what will happen, good luck.

Jorge from Visalia
It all happened so fast. Come to think of it, has anyone seen my prom date Jasmine?

Hannah from Dunfermline
Who are you!? What's going on!? Where is Noah!?

Sean from Cambridge
It feels like I am losing more and more of myself each day.

Paxton from Ogden
Maybe these people will turn against you Gabriel for creating a museum instead of leaving the dead alone.

Katie
Who are you? What are you? Leave these poor people in peace you monster!!!

Lauren
I'm excited and nervous... can't decide which one is winning!!

Erin from Pensacola
is this place haunted?

Fumika from Singapore
WHAT IS THIS :(

Lauren from Chicopee
Can't wait to meet the poor spirits of this school

Taylor from Tauranga
Incredible museum, so shocking to learn about this school's tragic history. Probably wasnt a good idea to bring my children here but hey, hindsight or something.

Chelsea from Corby
I knew a girl that had a sister who went to this boarding school!! Her sister was brutally murdered by the prom king and queen! There's a rumour that if you go to Lonesome Woods Boarding School on the anniversary of the prom massacre you can hear the dead screaming and the ghosts running around, the prom king and queen possess any human that enters to massacre even more!!

Destinee from Chicago
What's going on? I'm scared.

Alexis from Long Lake
So excited to read this book! Thanks for the help Gabriel. Keep giving those souls a voice!

Wendy from Alliance
Hey Gabriel, I got my school supply list, why do I need Holy Water, salt, crucifix, and a first edition copy of Malleus Maleficarum?

Ashlynn from Hickory NC
Noah is mine. Be warned doc. I'm coming for both of you.

Jack from Lonesome Woods
If Noah dies I die <3

Lauren from Atlanta
Ooooooo! I'm ready for this!!!

Angie from Black Creek
A little cooky and creepy, but what museum isn't? It's totally normal that you feel like you're being watched...right?

anamaria from croatia
I travelled so far to visit your museum and I'm speechless. I don't want to spoil anyone's visit, but visit it as soon as possible!!

Victoria from Stirling
If Noah dies, we riot.

Semera from Newport
love you gabe, see you soon xoxo

Loki
My pa always said ghost weren't real. He's dead now. Also, I got lost and ended up here, so hi?

Emma from Durham
Eagerly awaiting the tales from Lonesome Woods !

Rebecca from Somerset
Hmm...I don't think Gabriel is innocent in all of this Elliot, be careful who you trust. Remember, even though Noah is young and impressionable, he helped you become who you are today. Trust him.

Casey from Summerville
I'm excuse me, where are we?

Marcus
Sometimes healthy people only become mad through wrong therapy...

Emma from England
Urm... ok

Krissy from Walled Lake MI
Hello it is Krissy ♥ I'm looking forward to this book. Have a wonderful day! Thank you

Ashlynn from Maryland
May they all find peace.

Kelly from Marion
Not all souls who wander are lost

Shelbie from Cumming
NOT A CULT!!

Kelly from Marion
I'm so lost is this lonesome woods museum..where is it how do I understand it please help

Nicole from Madison
Very intriguing tour! Gabriel is very charismatic and knows how to keep a crowd interested! Just remember, don't stare into the void if you don't wish for it to stare back :)

Tanya from Helsby
Who are you Gabriel? I'm worried about Noah and Dr Harper and I'm coming to investigate this museum...

Charley
something tells me I should be scared to see you Gabriel

E.j
I can't believe no one believes me!

Jennifer from Gainesville
Hahaha it's funny that people still think that Timothy is missing!!! I know exactly were he is....

E.J from Hartford
Umm...I'm found? Hey, I've been waiting for someone who isn't Gabriel...he's not who he says he is..(*dabs with the biggest smile* hey!)

Maddie
Please help us Dr Harper

Robin
I don't know what this is all about but as a long time fan- I'm in!

Lee from Orting
I was a student I for less than a year. There is more is so much more to what happened on this property and no one is talking about. If you just take the time to research you will see. Its funny that the website shows blood dripping down the screen since its something that I personally saw while there. One night I was dead asleep and woke up to something on me.. as I turned my head there was blood

Anna from New Albany
What happened to Noah?! Give him back Gabriel!

Kaetie
I applied to teach at Lonesome woods back in the day... Guess that worked out for the best.

Tyranny
The museum is shit. Don't know why anyone bothers to upkeep this bullshit, it's a goddamn hoax.

Pixie from LA bitches
I started that fire and they deserved to die

The from Inside The Hall
Beware, beware, horrors are near, Trust your instincts, you should fear; Turn your back and you may die, The one who warns does not lie.

Tina from Larkhall
You better not do anything stupid Elliott. I will be watching....

Heather from Cleveland
Hi bye.

Kay from Wishaw
Gabriel is the love of my life

Katie from Pather
My visit to Lonesome Woods was made better by Gabriel,

Ashley
Gabriel, I know it was you who whispered "Get out" in my ear today while i was on my tour of the grounds. I mean, I didn't see you when I turned around, but it was most definitely you. Right?

Someone from Hell
H

benji from birmingham
i am just here amongst other people hoping that noah is okay, he better be okay):<

Elisha from Lonesome woods
Can't wait for tonight it's going to be so fun! Oh wait haven't I done this before? Never mind hang on what's he doing? Why does he have that knife? Oh no it's happening again! ......When are you coming home? It's cold down here you promised Can't wait for tonight it's going to be so much fun! Oh wait haven't I done this before? Never mind hang on what's he doing? Why does he have that k

Jexxi from Night Vale
The Spring Peepers are peeping deep in the lonesome woods. Peepers. Peep. Wahoo Cockatoo.

Orly
Hi Gabriel. nice name.

Joanna from Antioch
Dream? Nightmare? Either way I'm bringing a flashlight. Seems like it's going to be dark.

Elyse
Um Gabriel? Do I look like I'm going to fall for your shenanigans? A museum

you created to pay homage to lost souls...that's just asking for trouble. Oh, who am I kidding!? I look forward to joining you on this wayward trip of freakish happenings. See you soon!

billie-jayne
I miss Noah :((((((Gabriel do be killing all us students doe

Rebecca from Rotherham
There has always been something haunting about this place. Long before the stories you have to tell. And sometimes, the ghosts of all the secrets we keep, scare us the most.

Kira from Fayetteville
Kira was the most evil of them all. She cared for no one or nothing.

Tori from Lumberton
This is unsettling ...... I CANT WAIT ♡

Adrian from Louisville
See Ty... I told you this was pretty interesting

Nikki
Gabriel why won't you return my calls?

Ellie from London
Help...please...someone??

Rae
Tbh noah is hot asf

Gwendolyn from South of Kansas City, MO
Hey Doc, Noah is precious. You best keep him safe. :)

Olivia from Brighton IL
Dear Gabriel, You are not very good being the voice for all of us. LEAVE

Blaise from The Back County
I'm ready to explore the Lonesome Woods Boarding School. So awesome!

Melanie from Boston
This isn't what you think it is.

Julie
Where's Noah?!

Ashleigh from Patterson
Dr. Harper books are the best!

Britainy
Can't wait...

Kav from Lonesome Woods
This is some truly creepy shit...

Mistanie from Phoenix
Hi there, Gabriel! Looking forward to seeing your museum. But seriously, where's Noah? What did you do w/ him?!

Janaya
I don't know who Gabriel is, but I need you to leave me alone.

Gwen from Cairo, NY
Are Elliot and Noah alive? Do the fans need to come for Gabriel? Or are we all working together? Either way, I'm here for it.

Ellie from Ontario
I wonder what will be in store in this crazy messed up tale. Hmmmm...

Alexander from Ocala
Just when I thought it couldn't get any worse than the burger incident....

Samantha from Pulaski
It smelt like fire the whole tour. If I didn't know any better I would've thought the building was going up in flames.

Crystal from Massachusetts
Can't wait to meet you all again

Nurse from Boston
Gabriel and Dr. Harper, I signed that nondisclosure agreement for a reason. Those poor children, and their families, do not deserve this.

Danielle from Lancaster
I thought we talked about your morbid obsessions Gabriel...I hope your psychiatrist prescribes something useful. Like cyanide.

Lindsay from Memphis
Curse this school. I'm still looking for my sister.

Maire from Mansfield
I've got a bad feeling, I'm no stranger to that, but something here just feels wrong.

Dash
Ten minutes without a guide. That's all it took. Lost, hungry, scared. Oh look! Cooked meat, a little old, a little burnt, but it's something. Something to keep away the insanity. Someone please help. Why does this school look familiar yet distant? Didn't there used to be a dorm there? Have I... been here? Did I ever leave? ... Help

Bradly from Jessup
Here is Cowboy Death

Tiffany from Louisville
Woah who's Gabriel? We want Noah...

Aaliyah
Good evening Gabriel, I'm intrigued to learn about the story line of the Lonesome Woods Museum. What is your most favorite tragedy?

Madeline from Champaign
HEy, Looking forward to suPper this weekend

Claudia
I don't believe in hauntings but this is spooky shit! Count me in!

Brittany from Lavonia
I'm not used to things like this. I'm used to a small town, few people.. not cults.. murders.. These people deserve to Rest In Peace, not be exploited for monetary gain.

Kia from Phoenix
Sticks and Stones can crush my bones but Ghouls and Ghosts can never hurt me!

Renee
I can't wait for this!

Oscar from Around
Tell me, Gabriel... Do you believe that hell was made to appear familiar at first glance? What might look like a school... a prison, an island retreat, a psyche office... might only be a facade to give its captives false hope? After all, when in hell, one finds oneself in communion with an odd swarm of demons...

JJ from Centralia
They will never know the dark thoughts that cross my mind when all is revealed.

Kornelia from Frankfurt
Glad to see you again.

Julia
Gabriel, you have to let go of them... I beg you.

Jean
Can't wait!

Perla from San Diego
I feel like I'm missing something... Did something get published after 'I'm A Therapist...' Book 3? I've been trying to fill in the gaps for like an hour, but I can't find anything.

Richard from Transylvania
You shouldn't have left your son alone with that man, Elliot. Try and run I guess?

Jessica from Cecil
Where are you Dr. Harper? Where are you?

Gemma from Nottingham
I can't believe I am really here! My friends think I'm crazy for coming but

Timothy is alive and I've got to find him before more people die! I'm the only one who can save him, and you.....

Alex from Austin
My fiancé and I had a great time!! Can't wait to return some day.

Jan
This should be fun :)

Gillian
Every year really seems to end with a bang

Brandye
Did... did you say haunted?

Page from Lancaster
Hello Gabriel, I'm currently researching boarding schools for my daughter Nora. I've heard wonderful things about your school and we would love to schedule a tour of Lonesome Woods.

Damiana from Molfetta
What's happening here

Lori
Hello Gabriel. I can tell we are going to get along just perfectly.

Ricardo from Houston
Looking forward to seeing the history from Lonesome Woods Museum and to learn more about the curator.

Tyler
Ooo

Amber
Signing in from Hawaii. I'm excited to go on this museum tour and can't wait to see if anything *creepy* will happen while I'm here!

Alison from Ballycastle Northern Ireland
Wishing you the best of luck! Stay safe!!

Nadia from Castle Rock
Gabriel what have YOU done??

Lauren
This was meant to be a day out at a museum with my family .. that's not how it turned out

Emily from Ottumwa
This is truly terrifying Gabriel what a horrible place thank you for shining light on it

Alie from Essex UK
There's more to this place than meets the eye... Watch your back.

Kelley from Winchester
Thank you for showing us around! It was very informative to learn the history of what happened here. We really appreciate you allowing us to spend the night due to the storm. Can't wait to get home and tell everyone about you and this place!

Rachel from Haligoolah
Decided to visit the museum while on a road trip with my fiance. We love learning about "boarding schools", and love that Gabriel has been such a hands on host. Come to think of it... he's been a little too hands on. Where is my fiance?

Sean from Ventura, CA
As a nurse who has worked a multiple mental hospitals, I am dying to hear about a possible contagious mental illness. After witnessing *all* the different things that can happen in a psych unit, this honestly wouldn't surprise me too much.

TeeKayy from Fort Mitchell
I trust you, Gabriel. Just like those lost souls, my life is in your hands.

Teigan from Ipswich
This is weird. Where am I? This can't be happening. I have to get home, go away Gabriel I need to get home where's Noah? He'll take me home. What have you done to him!!!

Arian from Australia
This is why my mum never sent me to a boarding school...

Finny from Harrisburg
Hi, Maybe someone that comes across this can help me. The Dormitory collapse wasn't an accident. I've been working on this for years and no one seems to believe me. There's this guy Gabe (or is it Gabriel?) that I've been finding in some documentation I've reviewed from the investigation, but something about him doesn't add up. Maybe you can figure it out? Can we consult?

Hayley from Bethnal Green
Am I psychic or psycho? Guess I'll never know hahahaha

Jillian
WTF Elliot? Where the hell is Noah?! This is some bullshit!!

Henry from Washington, D.C.
My dad's uncle's wife says he knows Timothy Small and where he is. I promise you this is not trolling LOL. For realz!

Madison
Gabriel, Can't wait to see you again, I simply can't stop visiting the museum! I can never quite get it out of my mind...

Elizabeth from Cleveland
Just here to make sure Noah is okay... he IS okay, right?

Cadence
Is this real?

Jenny
No Gabriel please...you've taken it too far this time!

Roma
I see dead people.

Bethany
What happened here? Why a museum to commemorate such tragedy?

Dallas
Hello Gabriel. It is lovely to see you again.

Leon
Ugh, I'm so ready to be going back to school. You would NOT believe my summer.

James from Auburn
Hehehe, well what a delight we have awaiting for us here

Mal
Gabriel....I know what you did

Jacob from pensacola
i'm in boot camp and my girlfriend did this for me

Aaron from Livingston
Shout out to Destiny and Brax!!

Elvin from San Antonio
What is this? Where am I? WHO ARE YOU?

Jessica from Melbounre
Ready and waiting for instruction

Leon
I just wanna be in a book lol

Ashlyn from Memphis, TN
Elliot ... you're wasting time with this Gabriel fellow. We all know who your true soulmate is. ♡

Megan
Shoutout to James, we are both confused on what this it

James from Derby
The principal pissed on my wife :(

Tycalyn
What's gonna happen to those lost wondering souls now

Amanda from Owensboro

So excited for this!!

dylan
WHERE THE FUCK IS NOAH?

Jaelyn
Let me out I'm sorry!!!!! Please

Samantha from Durham UK
I travelled at long way to visit and it did
not disappoint. This boarding school is
as haunted as it gets!

Farida from Rotterdam
Hello?? WHERE IS NOAH??

Amanda
You don't know it yet, but we've already
met before. I thoroughly enjoyed our
first encounter, and i will be seeing you
again soon.

Alex
Oh, Gabriel, can't wait to see you! Hope
nothing happened to Elliot or Noah
though.

Maya
sus

Liz from Havenfall
Is this the real life? Is this just fantasy?

random
lets see

Lauren from Sunderland
Hopefully not the last book I'm
mentioned in

Milly from The Pack
Some women fear the Fire. Some
women simply become it.

Britney from Syracuse NY
These books are so wild and awesome!
Can't wait to see what's going on here

Rachel from Martin
Looking forward to a visit to the
museum!

Rachael from Plymouth
UK Resident ;)

Ruth
I think someone left the door open? It's
really cold..

Bobbi from Ohio
A pill a day keeps the mental health at
bay.

Vania from San Antonio
What is happening here?!

Kayla from Dallas
Certainly an interesting idea, love to see
if there's truth to the "hauntings"

Lindsay from Memphis
If you're reading this then it means that
after what feels like years trapped here,
my message finally reached someone.
Stay far far away from here. Tell my
sister I love her. I am lost, forever I
believe. Just run. RUN. I hear him
coming. RUN

Le'Niesha from Houston
Best museum ever. Had to sign this
guest book or I'll be haunted. Dr.
Harper is a wonderful doctor and We
love yu Noah.. shout out my son Omari.

Stephanie from San Francisco
Le Sigh... If only there were more
people like you (Dr Harper and Noah) in
real life...

Emily
Timothy went missing on a Tuesday... it
was always on Tuesdays

Leanne from Rochester uk
I need some more of those burgers star
boy

Pippa from Rochester uk
Gabriel tell momma to put the books
down

Olivia from Wonderland
Wow Im so excited to enter the

museum!!!!!

Alexandra
Woah...talk about an existential crisis. Is this what fictional characters feel? Hey reader, you look kind of ugly from down here. What are you doing? Hey, WAIT, DON'T TURN THE PAGE, PLEASE, I TAKE IT BACK, I CAN'T BREATHE IF YOU D-

Ais
Can't wait to see what happens :)

Alex from Berlin
I'm gonna cry if this actually shows up in the book ngl

Alicia from Sharpsburg, Md.
I can not wait to visit this new case.

Tamera from Wooster
This is a very interesting place, many of the children were so helpful and very considerate when I got turned around and lost during my visit. Although I still can not find my way out.

Phoenix from Portsmouth
I have two questions, who on earth are these people and what in the bloody hell is going on here ?

Atlagirl
Love one, love two. Sorry for bothering you.

ttv/chronospidey
Here we go again :)

Lily from Prescott
I can't tell who is real and who isn't anymore... all of the blood... the cackling laughter in the walls... every time I try to leave, something or someone keeps me here. To anyone reading this... leave immediately, and save yourself. I'm slowly going mad, and you will too...

Jess from Ann Arbor
Guestbook entry *

Henry
★★★★☆ weird sounds at 3AM, overall great place

Emma from New York
I'm absolutely terrified, but I need to know! Why do I do this to myself?!?! Is Elliot ok? Is Noah ok??? I need to know!

Cassie
Please leave us alone, we're just normal kids.

Yulissa
What are we doing here...? Who's Gabriel...? Is Noah ok...? He better be or we're going to have some serious problems

kay
don't you dare fuck with noah.

Jenny from Indianapolis
Can't wait for this! Morbid is as morbid does!

Mena from Sparta
i am excited as usual to read your new book.. interesting and weird but always i am curious about what you will write next.. thank you for writing something outside of the box for those of us that aren't offended by your MIND ???

Kai from Bradley
I can't wait to know this story.

Annie from Wellington
Gabriel... is that really you? It can't be, I attended your funeral just two years ago.

Allison
Very excited to see where this goes.

Haz from Exeter
Just had a lovely visit to the museum. Very lifelike, but a little too interactive. I felt like I was being watched constantly...

Charlotte from Teesside UK
Noah?! Where is Noah? What have you done?

Lena from Terre Haute
Gabriel....it's been a while, Gabriel. Are you still up to your old tricks, Gabriel? I've missed you so much. It's nice to see you've made something of the past. I'll come to visit you really soon, Gabriel.

Brett
Dr. Harper go home to your husband, son, rescue dogs and cat right now. Seriously. That's your happy ending.

Lindsay from Amelia
Hello? Dr Harper?? Can somebody please explain to me what is going on and why I am here?!?

Reese from Durham
Happy to be here, don't make me change my mind!

Romy from Munich
Romy was here

Peach
Thanks for the wild rides. -Peach

Alice from from leicester
marry noah. else i'll start a riot

Evan from Aberdeen
I like touching rusty spoons

Isabel from Overland Park
This museum exploits the children and families effected by these tragedies.

Ashley from Virginia Beach
Ashley had been gone many years and her soul was still not at rest in this museum that is full of lost souls.

Peach from Austin
The stench of death and a sense of dread hits you before you even enter. Entering this place was a huge mistake, probably my last.

Abbie from Hartlepool
Not sure what's going down in lonesome woods but can't wait to see what Dr Harper's going to do about it

Ginly from Lonesome Woods Boarding School
Tim isn't missing. He's dead. I know what REALLY happened in 2006.

Chloe from Inverness
Hello, Gabriel... I'm not sure how or when I got here! One minute I was lying on my bed reading a book and now I'm here in this boarding school I'm worried that maybe these books are coming to life or that I am in the book! (Ps love ur books)

Elizabeth
Sounds amazing, can't wait to read it!

Phoebe from Derbyshire
I visited this place with such high hopes, but I was so disappointed all I saw was magic tricks and a dinner show. Well that is what I thought until I got home, please help there's something in my house !!!!

Swepston
Elliot, you are too kind.

Bryan from Lonesome Woods
I grew up here and let me just say... Damn I wish I knew something was going on before it turned into a shit show. There's gotta be some weird curse or something. I'm tired of watching people go crazy or die.

Karl from I worked with damn Gabriel
Damn kids thinkin there's ghosts and demons and curses. No. Fuck off. Gabriel is the real fuckin nuisance. He's behind the entire god damn weird shit that keeps happening round here. I'm packing up and leaving, you idiots can either look at what's right in front of ya or you can keep thinking it's ghosts.

George

I remember my school's first cult :)

Melsiye
ehhh gabriel doesn't give off good vibes, seems a bit sketch to me :/

Massiel
Let's be clear, I did absolutely nothing wrong. I'm not to blame, it's not my fault.

Mercy
God has favorites and it's not me

Rogue
I hope that we meet in another life

McKenzie from Ashtabula
Dr. Harper you are amazing!

Jessica from Cecil
Why hasn't the screaming stop? It was supposed to stop. They told me it would. Why? Why can I still taste the blood? Where is the blood? I need the new blood......

Katiya
Oh Gabriel, it was nice seeing you. We have to hang out again sometime ok?

Jazzi
La Puissance toujours

Jordan from New Orleans
I've been so excited to visit this museum since the moment I found out about it!

Erin from Derry City
Wait... Gabriel? ... What have you done with Noah? A-And Elliott? WHERE ARE THEY?!?!

Veronica
Who are you?? Where is Noah???

Chyann from NYC
I am excited for this adventure, to my sons mommy loves you!

Dr.

Elliot, we've talked about this... You can't save everyone. Ruth worries.

Gudrun from London
Every Elliot needs a Noah.

Gemma from Leicestershire
Gemma Fitchett was ere

Leanne from Hell
I was supposed to be Prom Queen.... That bitch stole my crown!!!

Elliot from Knoxville
My husband Brandon and I have been following along together - super excited for the coming adventure! Much love!

Riley from Chesapeake
Came here to visit to see what my next school would be like! Thank you, Gabriel for a very informational tour of the school and campus. See you soon!!

Jessica from Kunsan, Korea
Lonesome Woods is not so loathsome it's a place where people go to lone souls to some who may need them. Enjoy

Leigh from Louisville
I'm famous!! In your face Scott!!

Clare from Bangor Northern Ireland
I can't find my sister, Kaylee. Does anyone know where she is? We got separated. We were told not to go down that corridor, but there was a loud scream and we ran. I don't know when I realised she wasn't beside me anymore, I thought she was there as I could still hear her trying to catch her breath beside me. When I reached for her there was nothing. But the breathing continued.

Carly from Wildomar
Whom the fuck you Gabriel :'(what is this all about I am scared and cold

Gary from Belfast
The defilement of my soul, still yearns

for the pieces of your heart. The darkness in your eyes, belies the levity in your smile. I miss you.

Clare from Bath
I need Jacob and Lottie to know I love them. I can't come home. I will always love my children but I must stay. They won't let me leave. I can't leave. LET ME LEAVE!

Caitlyn
Thank you for the wonderful memories! I cannot wait to come again ;)

Grace from Frankenmuth
Happy to be here! I hate school though

Nova
Absolutely lovely.

Dan from Doncaster
Really enjoyed the tour, can't wait to bring the wife! Thank you

Martha
Strange happenings occur here. Head my warning and be careful!

Kathy
I love you Adrian x

Morgan
Hi! My name is Morgan and I am glad to be here.

Ashley from Caseville
What on earth happened here? What happened to Timothy?

Sarah from Racine
Hey Gabriel! This soul needs a home. Any vacancy?

Gemma

Danielle
Thank you very much for allowing us to wait out the storm here. Can't wait to get home and tell everyone about the wonderful history this place has! Going

to recommend it to all my friends.

Anna from Liverpool (UK)
Little bit freaked out by the blood I see dripping down the page! Interested to see what road this takes me down

Cristyn from Mobile
Thank you Gabriel for trying to help me find my voice again

Ashlea
Gabriel? Where am I?

Haley
So excited to read about this place just the little details already given I can tell this one is gonna be a hard one to put down!

Shannon from Leicester
Enjoyed my time at the museum, Gabriel was great showing me and my friends around. Although I have a strange feeling I left with one more member to my party than I arrived with.. How odd?

Jade from Portsmouth
Gabriel, can't wait to read your work. Just one request, if you meet someone called Noah on your travels please please be kind to him

Leona from Newark
Looking forward to visiting the museum. Seems like it'll be a blast!

Minda
This place always made me feel uneasy, yet I never entirely wanted to leave.

gilly
love is not only what you desire

Jess from Devon
For my partner Harrison, who got me through lockdown by reading Dr Harper to me via FaceTime X

Lisa from Locust Grove
So excited, hope we make it through

Dannii
This place is strange!

Samantha from Florin Vineyard
And here it is, in black and white—proof
that I existed, and shall forevermore,
here in these pages.

Rosie from Dartford
this place kinda sus tho- oh well vibes ig
;)

Amanda from Redlands
Stay conscious of the liminal spaces
Gabriel. You don't realise how much
time you spend there. Nothing has
cameras for eyes.

Sophie from Northampton
Gabrielle? Elliot? Noah? What's going
on?!?!?

Jimi from Oxnard
I can't wait to see what's in store for us,
we're all just paper cut survivors,
anyway.

Shell from Northampton
Damian, Sophie and Charlotte- more
than the sun, moon and stars...

Taylor from Texarkana
Taylor, pls forgive me for getting you
into this. I meant no hard. Your best
friend, Jimi.

C
Gabriel, do you remember what
happened in Constantinople? I do and
soon everyone else will too...

Maya
Wonderful experience all around, would
totally recommend. Very inclusive
experience!

Chloe from Belfast
Hi, I may the next serial killer :)) and I'll
need a therapist

Amy

Thank you so much for the tour Gabriel.
Absolutely fascinating, you're doing
such a great job can't wait to return
when I'm back in the area.

Keleigh
hi gabriel , miss you and hopefully your
not to scared :)

Tiffany
Hi Gabriel! The voices in my head arent
anywhere near as bad as they used to
be and for the most part I can ignore
them......except that
one....certain....voice.....

tofu from dartford
woof woof *in a suspenseful way*

Brittany from Lavonia
Everyone who tries to help dies,
everyone who comes here is cursed.
Don't come and try to save us. It's
better if you left well enough alone.
Suicides and murders happen for a
reason.

Angelica
Maybe you can leave these poor souls
alone or just help them move on?
Instead of turning their resting/haunting
place into a attraction? Just some food
for thought.

Lucy from Norwich
If any iconic characters get killed off, i'm
going to be pissed

Olivia from Chicago
I hate it here. I wanna go home!

Scott from Liverpool
Followed your stuff from just after
Shooter was finished. Great to see you
back, and look forward to reading!
Hope you and Noah are both okay!

Tina from Vancouver
I'd like to leave now please.

Taryn from Lonesome Woods
Gabriel, I can't believe you've done this

to all of these beautiful souls, including mine. I hope the consequences catch up with you soon...

Hannah
Hello Gabriel, I do so look forward to this museum of yours!

George
I'm not as quick witted as the rest of the wonderful people who have written some great entries into this guestbook. Best wishes.

Macauley
Did anyone else hear a strange noise in museum? It sounded like it was coming from beneath me.

Michaela from Indianapolis
Noah was right you can really feel the creepy vibes here. I think I even met a ghost named Gweneviere she was so spooky

Jacob
I haven't spent a long time there, but I've always heard what has happened... I learned it's best to watch from a distance.

Donna from Napavine
Wow Gabriel! Thank you for everything, what a great place to see.

Evelyn from Qarafa
The lost souls won't remain lost forever...

Tracy
I survived Lonesome Woods Boarding School 💀

Marissa from Houston
I'm so STOKED!

Diane from Peterborough
I am looking forward to meeting you Gabriel, can't wait to see what you have in store for us !!!!!!! But I need to know WHERE IS NOAH ?????? Dr Harper you are amazing

Michelle from Chandler
You have my son Brayden and I need him back.

Yvonne from Musselburgh
That was interesting

Alexis from Southampton
Gabriel, it's good to be seen.

Dakota from Hell, MI
Gabriel- great museum! You should consider renting out to private parties, could be a great place for a reunion, company retreat, or wedding!

Yvette
Haunted boarding school? I am intrigued...

Andrea
Accident? Definitely arson! There's no way that was an "accident"... Wonder what reports are saying...

Kai from New Brunswick
What have you done with Noah?

Lindsay from Napa
Oh, but there's more you don't know. Nobody really knows all of it. Except me. I know all of it. They told me. I can tell you. Maybe they won't let me. Ask me. If they let me, I will tell you...or maybe I won't. Once you know all of it, it's over.

Lile from Aurora
I loved learning about the history of the museum, can't wait to learn more! I bet it would be quite fascinating to go there..

Kai from East london
While i was staying I saw the ghost and His 6 wives what a lucky man . Wait what that sound it just Arsenal Fc winning the league

Gina from Moncton
I don't understand Gabriel. What's

become of Noah? Why have you
brought us here? Please help.

Jo from Derby
What a fantastic series of books, Dr
Harper. I am looking forward to reading
all about Lonesome Woods...

Jennifer from Charlotte, NC
I sent all 3 of my boys to Lonesome
Woods Boarding School, only one
returned. I will be coming to find my
other two next week. I won't leave
without them.

Kayla from Chicago
Looking forward to meeting you
Gabriel!

Sammie
Great place to visit! My husband and I
love creepy things, it's just very cold...

Aishah from London
A very immersive experience - wish they
had a cafe that served iced coffee
though I was hanging. loved it
thoughhhhh

James from Lonesome Woods
The curse isn't over. He's always
watching me. Why did my dad send me
to this school?